He, Felt Scurrility

A Novella
& Four Stories

By Solomon Deep

Perpetual Imagination
Boston • Northampton • New York

881 Main St #10
Fitchburg, MA 01420

info@perpetualimagination.com

Manufactured in The United States of America.

10 9 8 7 6 5 4 3 2 1

ISBN-10: 0615730833
ISBN-13: 9780615730837

Library of Congress Control Number: 2012921903

This is a work of fiction. Names, characters, places, and incidents either are products of the author's imagination or are used fictitiously. Any resemblance to actual events or locales or persons living or dead is entirely coincidental.

Cover Artwork   "Carl" by Sarah Holmes

TABLE OF CONTENTS

For J. Raposa

A remarkable artist,
a remarkable human.

He, Felt Scurrility

2

She thought of taking up smoking so that she could measure her life in something. She had smoked three packs of cigarettes, so that must have meant a day had gone by. She hated cigarettes. Digital time drifted as requirements and appointments fell through her grasp. She wandered in her fog for a long time. Days at a time passed, and with them mistakes built up and she managed to forget to take care of herself. There was absolutely nothing that was keeping her engaged in life, or anything for that matter.

Sitting at the local mall one November evening instead of going to her class, Lorelei gazed at her digital watch as the battery died. The liquid crystal display of the cheap timepiece flickered, and went blank.

The mall was deserted, and improvised instrumental interpretations of adult alternative music echoed through the empty hive, even through there were no stores in the building. Dim light and the poporo of popping corn drifted around the corner at the far end of the hallway signaling the only activity, the movie theater. The cone gaze of floodlights hung down upon the large tiled promenade, misty and barren between islands of fake ficus.

She looked up to see if anyone else was there to notice her time problem; her eyes were drawn to one figure on the outskirts of the wide hallway that she hadn't noticed when she arrived. Double exit doors and service hallways were scattered down the hall between eery dead stores. One turnoff in particular stood apart from all of the others. She only saw his face and his hand; the rest of his body was obscured by the wall he was standing behind as he looked back at her.

From where she sat, his skin looked like felt. His eyes were black shiny glassy orbs set deeply into his face. There were glasses in front of them, filling out his features. His head was round, and his straight mouth appeared to cut deep and wide into his face.

Lorelei's eyes were drawn to him as if she were looking at an abstract sculpture, but this was out of place in reality. She thought she saw him move a bit more out of the dark, small with the proportions of a woman. His clothes hung loosely, but his hands and head were deliberate on a strong foundation. Lorelei stood, and cautiously walked closer to him on the promenade. She passed the ghosts of stores filled with graffiti, lint tangled in the dirty industrial carpeting, fingerprints and sandwich wrappers on their sills. She could hear her heart in her ears, and feel the fabric of her slacks bunched in her hands. As she got closer, the figure appeared to be more and more like an unbalanced craft store project, and a bizarre vertigo washed over her. Was this little man a puppet? Was it a trap to lure unsuspecting children with a shadowy maniac hiding in the doorway to snatch her up? Would he let her go because she was much too old?

Ten feet away from the puppet, she stopped and stared. This man, felt and wire and foam, was probably placed as some sort of practical joke or mascot. No. Maybe he was placed by the owners of the mall to prevent people from wandering through it at eleven on a Tuesday night - so they thought someone was watching them. How had she never noticed him before? How did this look on the security cameras? Or on the practical joke program on television where she would see herself when they played it? Sorry, that wasn't her.

The puppet man remained where he was. He was a statue. He was a red herring. Lorelei placed her cool hand on her forehead and sighed.

What was this nonsensical hallucination? It was too much coffee on school nights. Or non-school nights. Or not enough going to bed early. Or not enough care on cleaning up. Or something. It was time to clean up, again. Time to talk with mom and - or at least face the professors and see what she can do to at least pass. It would be a lot easier explaining a one-point-oh as a bastard teacher than a zero - that was just not showing up at all.

The next afternoon in her bedroom she heard the faint whispering; the lips parted as the spittle webbing expanded and contracted with every opening of the vindictive hole. It echoed upstairs and through the hallway and under her door like mercaptan-laced gas that has come to kill you in your sleep. The attraction of the slumbery death was overshadowed by the unbearable smell. Lorelei knew her mother was standing at the bottom of the staircase, tapping her finger on the worn down wooden orb that sat atop the end of the banister.

It was a bright and crisp morning and Lorelei was studying herself in the mirror as she felt the weight of her mother bearing down on her.

- What mother?

- Lorelei, you have to leave...

- What?

- You have to leave - you have class in fifteen minutes and I am leaving, and I know how you get wrapped up in things and forget to leave sometimes.

- Yes, Mother.

There was a long pause. Lorelei counted. Seventy-four

seconds. The front door opened and closed. Her eyes danced back to the mirror.

Was it her nose that was too big? Was it her hair that was lazily hanging over her eye just a little too much? Maybe she couldn't see herself very well... Or the hair was too blond. Or it was another blurry Wednesday. The ozone must be low because it was hard to breathe, and that must be why she couldn't see herself the way she really was. There has to be something memorable about today because not a day in life should go by without it being memorable.

Lorelei walked over to her bed and looked at her journal which lay open. September 16th. "The cradle of yearning" was written three days ago. She should sit down and write something, but nothing came as she guided her short hair over her ear. A loud car hummed by outside.

When Lorelei finally left the small ranch house she shared with her mother, got in her small foreign car, and made it to the community college, she was a half hour late for adolescent psychology. It was her second class of the day. When class was over she had an hour to burn, so she spent it in the library with her journal in front of her. As she reviewed her writing, the words retracted meaning; the only meaning that remained was within the paper itself.

She wasn't sure what that missing meaning was. Was today something she dreamed up? Was last night? Everything she wrote in this notebook was certainly not a reflection of the days she wrote it. Nothing happened. She wrote that day's date as a drunkard might, slowly and sloppily, "September 19th." Then, "there has to be meaning in today." Then a pause. Then, "Wuthering Heart." Then, "Wretched Heart." Then, "Wretched Heart, Wrenching Eyes, Wuthering Heart." And then nothing.

She scanned the library and thought about the homework she could be doing, but it didn't matter; she knew she was careless. Her mother would be disappointed in her grades, asking what happened, and 'I don't know' would suffice, maybe 'the teachers hated me' or 'I didn't understand what was going on.' That would work.

'Fogginess. Fogginess,' she wrote, 'fogginess is what I feel when I wander through the streets with a wretched heart and wuthered eyes. I lazily and haphazardly walk through the halls of Four Solitary Pines Plaza until I approach someone cloistered, shielded, wordless. He wears his empty heart on his lips, stretching from ear to ear, in permanent seriousness. I can't travel here, but I do.'

She reviewed her words, and digested their impact. She continued to write in non sequitur - it reflected her experience from the night before in basic, short phrases, parsed in such a way that only she could understand. She used a thesaurus. She made alliterative couplets. 'Lethargic liberal,' 'capricious caper,' 'apocryphal acquaintance.' She wrote in a dialect she only reserved for this, phrases bleeding down the page that captured the moment she saw the felt man watching her loiter on private, desolate mall property. The heat of the moment, that dangerous feeling of catching a voyeur at their dirty tricks... It was good to be looked at by the artificial security man, even if it were only for a moment and he was a foam imposter.

"Let's get married," he would say to her, through the hush of the hallway, his voice sounding like a dusting cloth on the first spring cleaning.

"Why, let's! Yes, let's!"

"We will run away! Get in your car and drive so far!"

"Oh, oh!" she would respond ever so gently, so as not to scare him away. The fucking likes of it she would never see. The hour passed.

She was writing all this, and then crossing it out because she is nowhere near as creative and aesthetic to catch the attention of a man on a foggy-brained Wednesday during her class that she was missing. She wondered why she was so stupid. She wondered why, with such an easy thing to do, to get up and go to the class she was missing, she was so goddamn stupid. The stupid bitch she was.

It was too early, it seemed, but she left the library and walked to her car. It was already four. Four clocks told her that on her way out the door. Her final class of the day ended in thirty minutes and four clocks told her it was four and she had to get in her four-wheeled junk car to get to the Four Solitary Pines Plaza, french fry dinner in her cup holder compartment. Organization was the key.

Drive through fries and cheeseburger supper, and a jaunt to the plaza to eat and be lonely in the dark was the plan. The rumpled bag and a car door slammed and she was walking through what felt like misty fall air that wafted through the creases of her clothes and up her pant leg. She approached Four Solitary Pines Plaza and briefly appreciated its facade; deep vertically stacked bricks that jutted out of the front of the plaza like magnified grooves on a record. They were then spliced horizontally every foot or two, and sandblasted with rough gravel to break up the monotony of what would otherwise be an unnerving boring taupe. As she got closer to the mall, the door's overhang passed above her, and she casually observed a rusting white lawn chair tossed atop a ratty old mattress in a tangle of briers that had not been trimmed since she was young. This was not only the landscaping of the Four Solitary Pines, but of her discursive solitary mind.

It was already dark in the mall. This is why she liked it.

She made her way past plate glass showcases containing a variety of nothingness that she loved. She passed stores with wire racks topful of emptiness. Absent clerks awaited her command to help her pick out the latest and most fashion forward nothing that they kept behind the counter because of its utter expense and high demand among recluses like herself. She passed a kiosk featuring the map of the plaza, a three-sided monolith which showcased all of the nothingness of the plaza in four large halogen tubes, turned off and absent of any lithograph or architect's film which may give any visitor any possible clue as to what lay in this dead zone where time stops and inward focus begins.

The sprawl of sheer vacancy was blinding.

She walked past her favorite stores: used to be Megan's Apparel, once was Amour-Propre, hardly Charlie Habiliment's, and shadow of Coldwater's. There were departments. Escalators. There was glass, empty fountains, and sharp granite calling for her attention, screaming for deliverance. Lorelei was the only appreciator of this magnificent artwork of timely detail and heavenly consumerism. This was the new era of the old era. Emptiness. The fog cleared as she sat on her favorite wood bench facing a vast hallway illuminated by the same cones of floodlights, far from the movie theater. She embraced her homestead for the brokenhearted.

She opened the bag, and the sticky aroma of salty vegetable oil and sugary beef and cheese wafted up her nose. She bought large french fries, and three cheeseburgers. She thought she had only bought one, but who knows. She was hungry and she needed to fill up. She tasted the fries, crispy, salty rods of reconstituted goodness. The burger wrapper was thrown to the floor such as in a fit of lovemaking. It was time to ravish and ravage the moment and the impending doom of not having the right amount of food in your mouth, now. Now. Eat it. Fulfill the emptiness while the fog has retreated for the moment.

But she chewed. She chewed and slowed down as she chewed. She looked down as she chewed. A slip of blue paper torn from a larger one lay hastily folded on her seat.

This created a chasm in her whole existence. This was her space, her food, her emptiness, and if there was any chance that she could be any less empty because she was sharing the space, then what the fuck was she doing here? Stupid bitch!

The paper lay, and where it was torn white fibers poked aside the line of the tear revealing jagged white mountains flocked above the light blue haze hastily printed on the paper. She put her cheeseburger down slowly on the bench beside her. The sensitivity of her senses turned up, her nose, ears, and eyes drinking in the surroundings like wine. The scent of cigarettes and fall slowly crept up on her as she picked the paper up and unfolded it. Silence blanketed her, absent of smooth instrumentals and the popcorn of the movie theater on the other end of the mall.

There was nothing.

Neatly creased, the paper opened to reveal nothing. She turned it over.

"I come here, too - and watch you. We can be all things."

It was written in a neat magic marker. A concentrated and heavy sans that pressed down on the paper only slightly. There were no errors. There were no mistakes or misspellings. It was perfectly written as if it were rehearsed. Was this the writing of the killer hiding in the shadows? The Phantom Of The Four Solitary Pines? She looked around in front of her, and there was nothing. The plaza was at rest, and the hallway continued its exhale. She turned around in the wooden bench, her eyes trailing the empty storefronts ensuring that she took in everything around her. Standing behind her on the promenade, watching her ever so softly, was the puppet man she had seen in the hallway a day earlier.

He stood gentle, his button down blue shirt and chinos loosely hanging from a bizarre frame that seemed ethereally supported by gauze and plastic pipe. His hands hung at his sides, a ribbon of smoke trailing upward into a pillow of haze above his head from a cigarette he was casually holding. Lorelei slowly stood and turned her body around to examine the man standing before her. She walked over to him, and his head turned ever so slightly bracing for her reaction. She walked around him and moved her head close to his but kept her distance. She examined.

His skin didn't entirely appear to be made of felt. It was a tight felt. It was a felt that was so tight that it looked like skin. It suited him, and his complexion was better than any men she ever knew. His hair was human, black, feathered and straight in a side part that would hang over his face slightly if it wasn't styled so well. It looked careless, but clean. His eyes were not black buttons as they had appeared before, and he wasn't wearing glasses like the last time. He had large glassy eyes that seemed a little bit too big for his head. They hung in their sockets with felt slightly bagged under them so he looked depressed.

She still had the unbalanced feeling she had the last time she saw him. He had a nose that fit his face perfectly, but where one would normally see nostrils, there was just one small hole. She wouldn't have even seen it if she wasn't studying him so closely.

He had a mouth, and through the loosely parted lips Lorelei noticed a pearly and clear set of ivory white teeth. After noticing the teeth, she looked to his hands, but there were no fingernails. She smelled cinnamon and eucalyptus, and she wondered if it was him or his cigarette.

She stood across from him and was captivated by his image caped in the misty glow of the floodlight above them, the air tossed with cigarette smoke.

"I am Carl," he said. His lips, tongue, and teeth did all the work. Lorelei didn't expect the depth of his voice, the articulation, the sibilance that his pronunciation allowed.

"We can be everything..." is all that Lorelei could say in response. He smiled his puppet smile, his eyes becoming more glassy and intentional. This moment was magic; Carl was magic. This was an outrageous proposition. This was a completely fantastic moment. This was anything, and they were everything. As the promenade and the dusty mall exhaled again, any remaining fog that was hovering in the cobwebby confines of Lorelei's mind was blown clear of the valleys, and dew hung on the foliage in the warm sunshine.

"We'll be wonderful. You are beautiful. Let me take you and we can be."

"That will be wonderful. We can be," she replied, her voice shaking. She was trying ever so hard, her heart burning and his felt hand seemingly reaching into her chest and shaking it gently. She trusted this hand as she envisioned Carl shaking her heart, sopped in her oily black blood that had been choking it, and removing his hand infused and dripping vile glops of crude.

In reality, he just reached out his free hand, and Lorelei took it. It was surprisingly warm, and soft, and not clammy or uncomfortable. It was toast, hot cocoa, slippers, and home.

They walked back to the bench. Carl put the cigarette in his mouth, then put the half eaten cheeseburger into the crumpled, greasy bag, and put it on the floor beneath the bench. All the while, his other hand kept a firm grip of Lorelei's hand.

"I am Lorelei." He looked down into his lap. He was reaching in his mind slowly for an answer; something to pronounce his own grasp of this situation.

He took the cigarette out of his mouth, and held it awkwardly in his right hand. "I have been waiting to do this. So long. I am sorry it took so long. I feel like I am falling." His voice, masculine, seemed sullen and sacrificing.

"Me too! Me too. I feel like I am falling, too! Where are you from? Tell me all about you - " Lorelei responded, cutting herself off at the end. She sounded desperate. Silly girl, shut up and let him talk! Shut up. Shut up.

"I don't know. I don't know where I am from. I come here and I watch you, and I live here because it is easy. I go to Weber Park and watch the seagulls. I go to the library. I watch objects come alive that people neglected while they worked themselves to death... Don't let go of my hand," he requested. His eyes trailed from his lap to Lorelei's mouth. He seemed so sad, and yet Lorelei felt like his hand was pulling her out of the water she has been submerged in for so long. Minor chords were played softly, ringing through her chest as her skin trembled. This man was the most sincere, most perfect, most appropriate piece - she touched her breastbone.

"Is this serious? Real?" Yes. He smiled faintly. She wasn't

sure if this was as big as he could smile. Was it? Was this a real smile? It was a safe smile and she felt like dozing, swinging wildly toward contentment and comfort. When she picked herself up again, they were gazing through one another's eyes. Stars bobbed to the top of his pupils, and electricity replaced what was left in between. "We should go to Weber Park."

"Is it dark out yet?"

"It must be." She looked at her watch instinctively, forgetting that the battery had died. This instinct had long been dead inside of her, but suddenly it meant something. The optimism was overwhelming. Popcorn started popping again in the cinema.

Carl removed the cigarette from his mouth and dug it into the carpet beneath his feet with his canvas sneaker. Lorelei squeezed his hand harder and felt the foam under his felt skin compress like a sponge, a wire skeleton beneath was faintly recognizable in her hand. She kept her eyes on him to see if he noticed her intrusion into his anatomy, but he didn't.

They walked out into the evening, warmer and windier air violently bearing down on them and caking clamminess on Lorelei's forehead. She worried that the wind would take Carl away from her. How much did he weigh?

"I never come out during the day," he said. "I usually come out at night so no one sees me, and I put on other clothes so no one recognizes me."

"Recognizes you?"

"Yes. What I am."

"You are wonderful." She almost said beautiful, but she had

to watch what she said so she didn't sound desperate - didn't sound more desperate. They made their way to her car, and the beauty of the car and the moment was completely realized where before it was commonplace. The car faced north in front of a bank of garages with large logo decals long removed. The ghost of their image remained. The car was a small rabbit awakening in its cracked, grassy parking lot shire. She instinctively opened the door for Carl, unsure if he could do it himself. He was so fragile, it seemed.

He looked at her hand in his and slowly released his grasp as if he couldn't believe he could ever bring himself to do it. Lorelei felt her joints squeak to attention as she opened hers. It was a small tragedy in a miraculous sunset of a day. Carl sat. She closed the door. The metal felt like an amazing and harmonic opposite to the new warm evening as it still held on to the coolness of the day ever so desperately. She noticed her other senses, heightened and brave. The halogen lights in the parking lot hummed, even though the ones near where she was parked weren't even on. The crickets chirped in the unkempt foliage tangles around the plaza. It was dark, but she could see everything - where she carelessly drove the key through the paint of the driver's side door, the curling up of the dried street paint that outlined the parking spaces, and, yes, the garage doors. The air smelled of brine, sharp and milky.

She got into the car. Door, seat belt, and key. Ignition, parking brake, and shifter. Headlights.

"May I smoke in here?"

"Yes! You don't need to ask."

"Oh," Carl replied, and took out a crinkly package of cigarettes, carefully removed one, and lit it with a fluorescent blue lighter he had. When he breathed in, his shoulders moved up, and when he exhaled the smoke a moment later, Lorelei smelled chocolate espresso, nuts, and wine. She never smelled that before. Carl continued, "I can't drive. I can't drive because I can't get a license. I can't get a license because I can't learn how to drive. I can't learn how to drive because I can't go anywhere, can't sleep, and can't ride the bus. I can't see people. But, I would like to have a car."

"No. You came to see me."

"Yes, but I can't see people besides. I trusted you before I ever decided to see you. I also trust the thirteen year old that I see behind the plaza who brings me my cigarettes... But that will end someday soon. His name is Kevin. His mother hasn't realized that there is always a pack missing from her cartons, and he hasn't realized that I am-" and he just stopped. He looked at Lorelei, his big dark eyes wrapping around her, "...I am glad I found you, that's all."

Lorelei felt herself smile because she was cognizant of so much more, such as her dimples forming at the sides of her mouth.

They pulled out, and three minutes later she turned left and passed the wooden Weber Park sign. The park stood at the edge of the town, a hill with a walking track around it paved through with a dark blue-gray gravel. Lorelei parked the car at a shut gate, and let themselves out. The moonlight blew trees, boughs, and leaves, whispering to each other, dancing to and fro. Carl and Lorelei walked around the gate, and up the hill, and holding hands walked above the trees and saw the darkness and stars blanketing the Pacific ocean.

They walked in silence, the small sparks of the stars, the giant moon, and the shadows and reflections of trees and waves composing a lyric and transfiguring painting of the world and the universe. They reached the edge of the cliff, the warm air cupping up and rushing against the steep drop above the trees where Lorelei and Carl stood. She briefly worried that he would be sucked over the edge, but she held his hand tighter and she would never let him go.

He was the first to let go of her hand, but only long enough to light a cigarette. As she watched him remove the cigarette and light it this time, she imagined black wire around his wrists as if he were being operated by an actual puppeteer. But they weren't there. He moved automatically and independent. It was amazing.

"This is beautiful. I like it here on nights like this. It is so free and fresh and lovely and large. This is a place of peace." He said as he exhaled. She watched his tongue move in his mouth. She wondered what it was made from.

"This is beautiful. I never come here."

"No one comes here."

"We came here. This seems like it is everywhere we should be. When I was in elementary school, we would come here and the guide would teach us about plants and what to eat in nature, and we would weave vinyl string. Gimp they called it," there was a twitch in Carl's hand, "and the guide would tell us interesting facts, like if you looked hard enough to the south you could see a lighthouse in Oregon from here." Lorelei finished talking, looking herself if any slices of light passed in the distance. On this clear night, there was nothing but the moon and the stars and Carl.

"I don't know what any of that means... But it sounds lovely."

His hand moved up her arm, moved over her watch band, and back down. It stopped at the watch band again. He looked down at it, and then up at her eyes.

Lorelei began to unclasp the rubber strap and remove the watch. She had no idea why she was still wearing it, and the distraction completely removed the importance and sensuality of the moment. She was motioning to put it in her pocket, but Carl stopped her hand. He took the watch from her, and looked at it for a moment. He threw it into the night, the watch seemingly propelled not by the force he threw it with but rather as if a string pulled it from his hand, off of the cliff, and into the ocean.

The moment was fiery and exact. It was a miracle.

Their time that they were together seemingly dragged on through the night itself. They hardly talked, but sat and enjoyed their presence and their touch.

Eventually, the time came for her to bring Carl back to the mall and leave him at the complicated line of doors at the rear of the building.

"The night watchman is an alcoholic. He is another reason why I can exist here. He has seen me, but it doesn't matter to either of us, it seems," Carl explained. He opened his door, a heavy metal door covered in rust and paint chips. It was a seemingly inexplicable movement that left Lorelei wondering how he could be so strong to do that. How could he be so wonderful? The amazement in all of this.

She rolled down her window with the crank. "When do I see you again?"

"Soon. Soon. In three days. Come here and we can be together again and it will be great. The movie theater will be closed and we can just spend time together here, if you like. We went to my favorite place tonight, so next time is your choice."

"Yes!" She wished there was another way to say yes. Another way to tell him how wonderful he was. Some way to make everything work out and make all of the answers to how all of this is working out come into plain view. This will take some time, certainly, but the magic of all of this couldn't be rested. This was working.

Carl looked at his waist, fiddling with the tails of his shirt which came untucked in standing and sitting between the plaza and their walk. Strings of thread danced on his pants as he fondled the workings of it all. His mind was made up, and he walked to the car. He put his head through her window, and kissed Lorelei. Heat burned up through her chest and temples, through her ears, the first kiss she has received in so long, and this was so very much of what she wanted and needed.

The kiss. The kiss was nontransferable, and there was nothing like it she had ever experienced. It was warm, caring, thoughtful, and staggering. Carl just as quickly turned from the car, and closed the steel door behind him. Lorelei turned the ignition, and began pulling away. She wished she could watch Carl's figure as she pulled away. It was only yellow halogen light that kept her company as it passed through her mirrors, past her windows, and then smaller and smaller into the darkness.

It was only after the drive home sitting in her room that she realized that she was sucking on her fingers; her lips were chapped from running her fingers back and forth over them.

The next morning the sun shone and the clean scent of the world wafted into her being. She showered, and prepared herself for class. She collected her books. She organized. Her outlook was completely different. She made her way downstairs.

- Lorelei?

- Good morning mother.

The optimism in her voice, in her step, and in her completeness was unstoppable.

- Lorelei, I don't understand what you were out last night until two forty in the morning about. I was worried sick about you, and frankly I am not going to keep putting you up in this house without a job. I am not going to continue paying for your classes with nothing to show for it but horrendous grades, incompletes - I simply refuse to do it.

- Yes mother.

- Well, what can we do about it?

- Let's talk about it later. After class...

- That is even if you go to class, isn't it?

- I am going to class. I have two classes today.

- ...

- I am going now, but I am not angry.

- What does that mean?

- Nothing.

Lorelei left the house at exactly 8:15 that morning, and arrived at her class at 8:28. She sat through the class until it was time to leave, at 10, and then followed the professor back to her office. At mid-morning, the day was already hot, and they walked with sticky moisture dripping from their bodies. They discussed making up the work she was missing from the past three weeks, and that it was okay, and that she understood.

She walked to the library, fully intent on using the ninety minutes of her early arrival to work on makeup assignments, and also fully intent on attending her next class. Optimism rushed from the dam holding it back in her brain, and her mind switched from logical thought to logical thought. She sat in the library typing on the computers and making her way to the research books and returning to her things, all the while feeling like a migrating bird who was finally joining the flock if it wasn't too late. The caw caw of the clock and its ancient motor was the only reminder of time passing.

Since her watch battery died and her watch was thrown into the sea by her lover, she was surprised that the clock - maybe time itself - only served as the distant taupe face of the nothing that blanketed her life. She wasn't sure when her little heart began to ache so very badly and wrench her soul away from her with it, but now this atomic optimism has inflated her heart to absorb all of the wonder that she was finally careening toward.

Lorelei wasn't sure if it was time that was finally catching up with her, or herself catching her breath on her schooner traveling ever so quickly now on the sea of time, but the days melted away along with the amount of work that she had to catch up with. A stack of papers to hand in dissipated and disappeared from her grasp and into the possession of the licensed authorities on adolescent psychology. It was time to rest her mind and focus on the one true thing that she had to look forward to every day when she woke up now.

Carl.

It was seven in the evening, three days later. She drove past the neon liquor stores and payday loan shark storefronts up the broad avenue of route four. Two lanes of headlights passed in the opposite direction and screamed at her eyes as retail civilization dropped away little by little. Streetlights moved farther and farther apart. Pavement and parking lots grew broader, as did the cracks in their shallow skin that revealed soft, snowy green brush stretching upward. A Cadillac idled in one, awaiting a visitor. A pedestrian sulking and slumpy like the plastic bags he was carrying traversed across the broad forest of another. And Lorelei drove on, passing these sullen landmarks with a new carelessness that manifested itself from a completely different part of her mind. She finally had somewhere to be.

She pulled into the parking lot of Solitary Pines, eager to grab Carl, to sleep alongside him, to read with him, and to be completely content with the moment and with life itself. Acceptance has finally transcended into her mind through a new purpose. There were no cars in the lot. Everything was finally clear.

She drove around to the back of the building, passing much less than she remembered. It was dark, and the yellow halogen lights shone down on rusted doorways of heavy steel. She parked where she dropped Carl off, remembering that this door was unlocked. The shifter clicked up three positions, the key turned off the car, the car door closed, she pulled her weight against the heavy rusty door as it freed itself, and it scraped rough and grustly against the ground and its dry hinges. Cool air washed over her from inside, bathing her in comfort from the hot night.

Darkness hung. She was in a hallway. Faint light came from a small window of an industrial door at the end. She began walking, but felt like she was falling because of the endlessness and uncertainty of the moment. Her passionate heart beat in her ears, yet her frail body trudged confused like the feeling of stepping up for a phantom stair at the top of a stairwell. She floated, glided unsure, toward the golden faint light of the window. As she approached, she saw through to the golden light bouncing off of the faintly sparkling concrete wall on the other end of the hallway through the chicken wire reinforced glass.

She reached the door and felt its surface. She felt a push bar that resembled black coal in her hands in the night of the hallway. A bar of black coal. An oversize ingot of coal. She pushed, and entered the mall's promenade.

It took her a moment to realize what side of the mall she was on. She never came this way because of the people that would normally be bustling through to the cinema. The theater was to her left at the center of the bend of the mall. She could see a sliver of it from where she stood, and it was closed tonight - thin fogged plastic panels extended on tracks in front of it like vertical blinds held together with rods as a security precaution. There was only faint light coming from a single emergency flood around the corner, probably by the entrance. More faint golden light leaked from behind her.

She turned, and her eyes grew large drinking in the magic of the moment. Steel bars rose from the promenade to create a path of arches that lead to a center gazebo that was also a skeleton of steel. There were Christmas lights built into these structures, and the orange and gold light cast by them illuminated the hallway that grew distant. The ceiling pulled away from the scene, with fabric stretched across wire to resemble clouds, and more Christmas lights in the ceiling to represent stars. The ceiling and the walls moved farther and farther away as Lorelei walked closer and closer to the gazebo. Sitting on the gazebo's bench, plain, composed, and waiting, was Carl.

Lorelei arrived at the entrance to the gazebo, and Carl addressed her.

"Hi." He was smiling. Smiling a puppet smile that was remarkable. Or his head was turned just so. He was debonair. He was magic.

"Hi." Lorelei replied.

"I did this for you." His hand washed over the room, and then at the bench where a small tablecloth was laying over it and a bottle of red wine rested with cheese and crackers. "Come sit down."

Lorelei was smiling as Carl was, deeply cut into her face and almost traveling around her head. She sat. Giggled. Drank from the glass of wine already poured, and placed a square of cheese on her tongue and savored it. This is the most unbelievably amazing thing that had ever happened to her. The most romantic. The most unconditional thing. The most real thing.

"Lorelei, you are beautiful." He said. She blushed, pulling her chin into her chest. The wine was quick.

"This is so wonderful, Carl. This is so, so wonderful." They kissed, and it was so much more heavy than before; heavy with more meaning, substance, and miraculousness than before. Carl retreated, and as he did the angle of his face now looked like a frown, or at least deeply serious. "Why don't you have some wine with me?"

"I would love to," he began, "but it really doesn't do anything."

"No!"

"Yes. None of it does."

"Really? What about the cigarettes?"

"I just want them. That is all," he replied.

"And food?"

"Nothing."

"Well, what do you need?"

"You." She blushed again. He crossed his legs, lit a cigarette, and folded his arms so he held his elbows.

"Where did you come from," Lorelei asked jokingly, shaking her head. It was a rhetorical question that actually had an answer. Didn't it?

"I don't know, I tell you" he replied humorously, but the sullen and serious look seemed to return to his face. "I know we are together, and I know that we are still getting to know one another, but... But I finally came to talk to you for a reason." Lorelei followed closely. "I need to leave here and I can't come back, and I feel like you would be the one to protect me."

She hardly needed to consider it. "Of course! What is there to discuss! We will leave here tonight - only my mother... Oh hell, we will leave here tonight, and you will come home with me and we can just exist. Of course, you need to be extremely inconspicuous at my house. No one can know that there is a boy living there."

"Oh, I know,.... This is what I live with. It is okay. We can make this work." Carl's face changed to caution. It appeared worried. It wasn't changing at all.

"We work." Lorelei observed with a wrinkled brow and a smile.

"This is real." Carl observed as he took the box of cigarettes from his pocket and removed one. Lorelei observed his fingers on the hand he smoked with. There were notched grooves in his felt skin that were discolored. Lorelei grabbed his hand, removed the cigarette, and examined it.

"Oh, Carl, what is this?"

He shrugged, his hand held like he was at a palm reading. "It is heat. It is just heat. I am not made to take some things. It is okay; I think it suits me, I guess," he said, taking his hand back and taking the cigarette back, "...It is okay."

Lorelei looked at him, recognizing that she was beginning to be a crazy girlfriend, and to just let that go. He would have to stop smoking. He would have to, eventually.

"Well, can we be free now?" Lorelei said.

"Yes. Let's be." Carl reiterated, and they kissed once more. Carl placed a piece of cheese in Lorelei's mouth, and Lorelei took the wine. She drank from the bottle, and reached for the glass.

"Just leave it. It is okay." Carl added.

They walked under the iron arches, onto the promenade, and left down the hall toward the back door. Carl led Lorelei down the hall by the hand, and stopped her halfway. He held her waist, and kissed her. He moved her toward the wall, and kissed her. She leaned against the wall, and they kissed. Time crawled and Lorelei was entrenched in vigorous passion. She felt his hands on her body, on her neck. It was more magic. She was falling, again.

She drank more wine, and they got into her car and drove away.

When they arrived at her mother's house, they tiptoed through the kitchen, and Lorelei kept the lookout for mother. She was nowhere to be found, and they slithered up to her bedroom. The lights stayed off, and the stereo was turned on. This common evening activity was now weighted with such greater importance and such miraculous gravity. They kissed, and Lorelei's mind swung and spun from the delicious Cabernet.

They kissed and kissed and heaved and heaved. Their bodies were passion itself. Lorelei let it come. Clothes were tossed to the floor, Carl's foam body stiffening as he breathed; did he need to breathe? He was a fragile oval, not even a torso, one large piece of felt stretched over a confusing plush frame. She grabbed at his waist, pulled at the seams of his trousers, but he was persistent. Her skirt flew up, and she breathed hot as he worked feverishly at her. The rest of the night was a drunken blur, contentment waxed through a red wide haze and her reaching under her bed for the purple vibrator she kept there. The strangeness of his body, feeling down into his pants the pale, flat pelvis, the lack of any fold of skin to form an ass crack, the miraculousness of his animation was all completely overshadowed by the blunt romanticism that blinded Lorelei from the beginning.

The next morning, they awoke to her mother banging on the bedroom door.

- Open this door. Open it now. If you have someone over here I demand to know.

Emptiness. Neither Carl nor Lorelei spoke a word. A thumping headache crawled over her brain like a hermit crab.

- Open this door now, Lorelei. I demand an answer.

Carl sat up. They looked at one another, and then they both looked at the space between the bottom of the door and the rug. They were parenthesis, and mother was an expletive. Carl bounded into the sliding door closet, while Lorelei silently but quickly stood and found clothes to wear, her breasts bouncing and flaying as she desperately shimmied into a pair of dark blue jeans on the floor. She found a shirt, and slipped it on.

She reached over to the door, and opened it.

Her mother was livid. The veins in her eyes beat with lucid anger and disgust. She pushed past Lorelei and trod through the room as if the room were shaking with every step and contraband was sifting to the top of the mess. She stopped, looking accusingly and disgusted at Carl's shirt laying on the floor next to Lorelei's bed as if it were open armed for a great big hug. She closed her eyes.

- Lorelei, you are to move out of this house immediately. You are not to take anything but your clothes with you...

She was silent.

- Is that boy still here?

- No.

- That boy is still here.

Her mother said this and began trudging through the room again, pushing the mattress off its foundation, pushing her dresser over to see behind it,

- No, mother, no, please,

And she finally looked at the closet. Both of their hands shot toward the knob which pulled the closet open on its casters, a knob hardly built for one hand. Lorelei lost her grip, and her mother pulled with such force she hit herself in the face with the hinge of the closet and fell backward onto the box spring laying on the floor of the room. Carl watched all of it unfold with a startled look in his eyes, motionless.

Mother sat up, blood pouring from her nose, into her mouth, and down her chin slightly. She was baying lightly until she saw Carl, her expression immediately changing to that of horror.

- Get... that... get the fuck out of here. Get the fuck out! Get out!

As she gurgled this, Lorelei grabbed Carl's arm and pulled him out of her room, and they ran down the stairs and out of the front door. It was an unbearably hot morning. They got in her car. Lorelei started it hastily, and they drove off panting.

"Where do we go? Wheredowego wheredowego wheredowego?!?" Lorelei asked. Carl was riding silently in the passenger seat, catching his breath. As she drove, she noticed that he was looking down into his lap. "Carl. What is it? Where should we go?"

"We can't go anywhere. That was my shot."

"What was?"

"Nothing... Let's go to the park."

"No, let's go to the mall."

"No, we can't... Let's go to the park."

"Don't be ridiculous. We can go to the mall and sit and think for a little while."

They drove for twenty minutes. As they drove up route four, past the stores, then the pawn shops, then the payday loans, then the grassy parking lots, then up to the mall, there was one major difference. As Lorelei drove the car up the short driveway, she met a chain link fence. The parking lot had men with trucks unloading temporary fencing on concrete slabs onto the mall property.

"What is this?"

"It's why we can't go here. I told you, I needed somewhere to go." He paused, then looked at his lap. "This is it for me. I knew this would happen. There is nothing that I can do. This is awful." He reached into his pocket and removed an empty pack of cigarettes. He tossed them onto the floor of the car. Lorelei began to think that things were going terribly, awfully wrong.

"No... No this isn't it. This isn't it at all. This is nothing. I am just not sure what is going on here... What are they doing?"

"Can't you see? They are closing the mall; it was closed when you came last night."

"Yes, I can see that, but I can't see why-"

"Just - Can we go to the park?"

"Yes... Yes, I guess."

They drove to the park silently. Mid-day was creeping up upon them, and the air, the car seat, the steering wheel, and the seat belt buckles pinched at their skin and clothes. There was nothing comfortable about their present condition. Nothing at all.

They parked in the parking lot; it was still daytime. There were only two other cars in the park, and Carl felt comfortable. They exited the car, and walked to the edge of the park near the cliff where they were before. There was nothing amazing about the foliage. There was no fantastic sparkle or new color in the gravel. There was no majesty in the seas or the stars. Lorelei felt as though her moment of awe was slipping gently away. How much she missed those moments with Carl.

And yet, he was still here.

They sat, and the surf was still and quiet. The sun beat down on the pair. Lorelei was unsure of what to say, and she wished she could have stopped to get Carl cigarettes. Anything. At this point she would do anything to make it work a little bit longer.

"This is the end of it all, it looks like," he said.

"No, wait... What?" Carl looked at her. "Listen, there is something we can do. We can make this work. There has to be somewhere you can go - we have homeless shelters and -" She stopped, holding her forehead. She understood that it wasn't resources that Carl was in need of; it was humanity. She looked over the tops of the trees. "We are both going to need to figure something out. It is just that simple. We can do this." But he just continued staring.

There was a rustle of grass behind them, and three young men in hooded sweatshirts were walking toward them. Carl stood up. There was something odd in this gesture, as if there was nothing he could do in the situation, but he did it anyway. There was a pureness to it, just as the dangerous feeling in the pit of Lorelei's stomach engaged. Something was not right.

The shorter, black haired one began taunting him first. They were saying things, harshly, and laughing. They were poking his shoulder, and he drifted back easily - but he wasn't moving. He stood as firm as he could.

Carl said something back. They laughed.

What happened next wasn't entirely clear, but the boys splashed something in his face, and kicked dirt at him. Lorelei later observed that it appeared to smell like honey, but when they did it, it was more like a soft drink.

They pushed him again, he took two steps back, and they yelled at Lorelei,

- Go fuck yourself, bitch! Your emo boyfriend likes dicks.

They walked on, laughing.

Carl returned to sit by Lorelei. His face was sopping wet, and his mouth had a new downturned, sad, unfortunate overbite caused by the new wetness of his visage. He looked horrible, and Lorelei had to do something to remedy this. It was soaking into his chest.

"Carl, let's go back to the car. I have a towel in the trunk, and I think that we should-"

"I just wanted to come to the park," he was saying, almost to himself. "I just want to be with you. To be safe. Everything is ruined."

"No... no, Carl, what? No, nothing is ruined. We just need to have a new perspective here. We need a new plan. That's all..." He hung low as she took the hand of her valiant knight. She walked and he shuffled back to the car. He refused her towel. He just sat in the car. She walked around, put the towel back, and got in next to him. The air was thick with fructose.

"Carl, we can do this. Both you and I are without homes right now. We can do this!"

"You always have a home. I have nothing."

"You can't talk like this. Really. Listen, I am going to go talk with these people first thing Monday, and we will square away what is going on with the mall. I don't want it to go away just as much as you probably don't. That place is sacred to us."

"I don't care about the mall. I don't care about the mall! I care about being somewhere where there is no one. I care that I can walk around in my own place and not be bothered. But I don't care about the mall... It was just dark and safe. I wanted to be with you at your house, dark and safe."

"I never even felt safe there," Lorelei implored. Carl looked at her, exasperated. "Let's just get something to eat. We can get you some cigarettes, park at the KelMart and survive there for a couple of days, and see what is going on on Monday before class... That is all we have to do. It is simple." He looked at her. There was nothing in his eyes. He seemed empty. "We can do this. Trust me."

And they did.

Lorelei drove seven minutes up route four, and parked in the lot of the KelMart. She bought two bottles of Cabernet for three dollars each, a loaf of bread, a new shirt for Carl, and a small package of processed cheese singles. She got Carl two packs of cigarettes, and an application for employment to get some income for the two of them while they live out of her car. When she returned to the car, Carl was waving his hands, wildly. The windows were open, and she could hear the soft pat of his hands and elbows against the door frame and the roof of the car.

"What is happening!"

Black specks swarmed around him in the hot, dry day.

"Flies! Everywhere!"

Lorelei immediately went around to the trunk of the car. She removed one of the towels that lay underneath her materials for class. The books flew across the trunk as she spun toward the passenger side of the car and began to blot the syrupy liquid off of his face and out of his skin. He was still soaked through. She pushed the towel into his face, sopping up sugary drink. In his face, there was only a little padding, and the towel got much of the liquid out - but where it entered his chest, it seemed to have soaked inside. No matter how hard she pressed into his soft plush body, it was still wet.

For the rest of the evening, they were silent. Lorelei drank one of the bottles of wine, and it was too hot to do anything but relax in the car with the doors and windows open. She did some of her homework, and Carl chain-smoked his cigarettes. Lorelei wondered if this was the bulk of how he spent his time.

"Would you like something to read?" she asked.

"No. I don't read."

They stayed up until it was dark out. They huddled up in the back seat, and fell asleep.

In the middle of the night Carl awoke screaming, and in turn he woke up Lorelei who saw something gray scurry away from the open backseat door. Carl screamed and screamed, and was grabbing his face.

"The animal! The raccoon! The raccoon ate my face off! The flies ate my face off," he shouted. He was completely hysterical and almost incomprehensible. He mumbled.

"Shh, shh, shh, what?"

"The flies ate my face off!"

Lorelei calmed him down, reached into the front seat, and turned on the dome light. She persuaded Carl to remove his hands from his face. Horror. A gaping tear of felt and missing chunk of white foam stared wide-mouthed at Lorelei, as if someone took a giant, serrated melon baller to his face. Lorelei felt sick.

"Oh, oh Carl. Does it hurt?"

"No. But this is hideous. This is ridiculous! I was so much better off yesterday! Why do things have to change? This is horrible!"

Lorelei didn't know what to do, and her brain was still drowned in wine.

"Let's close the doors and the windows. I am so sorry," she suggested.

"No, we can't. It will be too hot in the morning."

"It will?" She felt like she could do nothing to please Carl. While her mind was now in the most stable, clear, and uplifting state of mind it has ever been in, she has never been more desperate to try to control a situation she felt she couldn't. Her hands were empty. Her eyes were wells of ungratifying cement. She was completely unsure of what she could do to prevent him from being any more miserable. "Can I... Possibly... Can I possibly have you stay in the trunk, then? And we can get up at dawn so it won't be hot in there, and I can make a bed for you..."

"No. No, I just won't sleep and I will stay up for the remainder of the evening and-"

"...and we can get a hotel tomorrow. Nothing like this can happen there."

He looked down at his lap, the shifting shadow of the crater in his face sparkling with tiny glistens of the polyurethane bubbles. He looked so, so sad at the prospect of existing.

Lorelei slept the night through, and they drove to a motel up the street. They spent the rest of the weekend there, watching television, laying in bed, drinking wine, eating bad cheese in cheap bread. It was an existence that would patiently usher them into the week that they could still break into the mall and allow Carl to exist there. Then their relationship would have a strong foundation, and all would be wonderful again.

Monday morning, they drove to the mall. The plaza was

completely entrenched behind a solid moat of chain link fence. They pulled the car up to the fence as they had before, and Lorelei got out. Behind the fence, backhoes, excavators, and front loaders filled the parking lot, and men with hard hats discussed what seemed like very important business.

"Hey!" Lorelei yelled. She looked back at Carl, who was sitting in the idling car looking at his hands in his lap. A few hundred yards away, three of the men in hard hats looked over, but returned to their discussion. Lorelei slowly removed her hands from the fence, and returned to the car.

"What are they talking about?"

"They are tearing down the mall," Carl responded.

Lorelei just realized that this was the likely end of it. It was so easy to go in and out the last few years. It was simple to sit, and leave trash, and eat, and not be bothered. The movie theater was all that was left, and yet last week it was closed for the first time. This was as long as Lorelei could remember. The heyday of the mall ten years ago was now a distant memory, and it was being torn down because it was over.

"Why?"

"Why do they do that? You tell me. Money, isn't it?"

"Probably. But, what do they expect you to do?"

"They don't know me. They don't know me at all."

Lorelei thought. Nothing came to mind. She thought so damn hard, but was empty of concept and comprehension. This didn't make any sense. This fate and this lifetime was just too damn much. It was too damn unfair. Magic had finally entered into her life and she had something gratifying to fight for, and this is just too goddamn coincidental to be happening right now to her now that she was so happy. Now that she was so goddamn happy.

She looked at Carl, this man who came into her life and who was exiled from his home. He was pathetic. A chunk of his face was missing, he was dirtied with soda and filth because of the world that doesn't like him. Well she liked him goddammit, and she would not stand for the sulky bowed head and attitude that has washed over him the past few days.

Carl's hands sat folded in his lap, his shoulders limp. She wasn't about to give up.

She shifted the car into reverse, and sped through four lanes of the oncoming traffic of route four, cars swerving and darting out of her way. One of her rear tires popped as the vehicle bounded over the curb and hopped into the empty overflow parking lot across the street from the plaza, sparks shining and hopping from the underbelly of the front of the vehicle as it landed. She stopped, pulled the shifter into drive, and slammed on the gas.

"No. No, no, no, no, no. Lorelei, no." Carl erupted.

Smoke billowed from the rear of the car. It hopped over concrete, back onto route four displacing more vehicles traveling in both directions, drove up the driveway, and slammed through the chain link fence. The right side of the car bounced over the concrete slab, more sparks, and a shining spiderweb suddenly appeared on the windshield with two concentric breaks echoing out from the center like a glassy pond rippling from two pebbles as the fencing clanged over the windshield.

"No, Don't do this," he implored.

Sparks shone in a wall as the rubber on her rear tire tore away to carry the vehicle on a bare steel rim. She kept her foot firmly on the gas, steering the car straight at the various construction workers. The hum of the engine struggled to keep up with her passion, and the workers darted out of the way. She cut the wheel, swerving the car right, and drove up to the front of the building between the construction equipment. The car carried them in a semicircle left around to the back of the building, the rear end swinging and dragging behind them on the instability of the one working tire. Rubber and fiery confetti darted and bounced across the pavement.

Driving recklessly past doors and doors, bottles and paper bags, garbage and graffiti, she arrived at Carl's unlocked back door to the mall. She clamored out of her car, pulled the heavy steel door of the mall open. It's dry hinges shrieked. She ran down the dark hallway straight into the emergency door, and it slammed open against the wall. Hopping a few steps in, she stopped and looked around her.

To her left the movie theater was bare and empty. She hadn't realized it when they had driven up, but to her right they had already begun demolition. A gaping hole in the western side of the mall opened up into the hot September morning. Just beyond their beautiful and homely steel gazebo and its romantic walkway was a pile of rubble that stood below the blue sky. She screamed, and her scream echoed on her left, and was muffled by the expanse of atmosphere on her right.

She had never been so sure of something in her life. She was going to save this mall, as dead as it was. It was a monument. It was more important than anything. She turned on her heels and ran back out in the direction she came in. Outside, Carl stood next to the car with the doors open and was rolling the windows up.

"Carl, I am going to save this place. I am going to stay here."

"Don't do that. Don't do this. This isn't important."

"No, no. Don't you want to feel safe again?"

"Lorelei, this place is being torn down."

"But you said."

"I know, but now it is dead. We can't come here because they are tearing it down. We can't go to your house because of your mother... And- Lorelei, this is ridiculous." As he talked, wisps of felt bobbed from the bowl cut into his cheek. He was shaky. That made him all the more real... important.

They were both frozen looking at each other. Lorelei began to think that this wasn't about herself at all. This was something that was so much more. Dignity. Justice. Equality. The new order of the remarkable love she shared with an obscure man. She slowly turned her head toward the door, walked back through it, down the hall again, entered the mall, and sat on a concrete bench. She wasn't going anywhere.

She wasn't sure how much time had passed, but hours seemed to drift by as the muggy hot air seeped through the wide, cavernous hole and surrounded Lorelei.

The groggle of diesel equipment could be heard.

This was it. It was the moment Lorelei had been waiting for. This was her figurative war on the deconstructive world. The undeveloping of development. The clear cutting of dead, safe space. What right had they!

A black and white skid loader came barreling into the mall from the hole. It was moving back and forth, picking up it's arm, dropping it and sweeping scattered pieces of steel, ceiling panels, glass, and plaster into the big pile. Behind the big pile, a mechanical arm picked up pieces of the mall and was dropping it off somewhere out of view. It made eight or nine trips before it stopped. The driver turned the machine toward Lorelei. It inched closer to her in the sunlight, but never entering the shade underneath the overhanging remnants of the ceiling.

It turned and sped out of the mall.

Minutes later, six men in reflective yellow vests and hard hats came walking to the hole in the mall and stopped. They were looking in. One pointed, and the rest cocked their heads and strained, not entirely sure what they were looking at. Another older and fatter one came barreling in carrying a bullhorn.

It clicked.

- Hey! We need you off of the premises right now. We have called the police. This is a dangerous work area and you are sitting under unstable roofing supports.

Click. His nasal cupped voice echoed down the hall.

"Stop tearing it down," Lorelei replied. They looked at one another confused.

Click.

- Lady, we couldn't stop tearing it down even if we wanted to. It's gonna fall down anyway. Now, get out of there.

Click.

Lorelei sat. She looked up at the ceiling. The foam tiles were crooked, and some had already fallen from the braces that had given way further down the hallway.

Click.

-Please, lady - we're just trying to do our jobs, and if you get outta here the police won't arrest you. If you get killed it is our asses on the line. We won't even come in there to get you, that's how dangerous it is, lady, so...

Lorelei's ears rang, drowning their voices out with whiteness and nothingness. She examined the pile of rubble dwarfing the men, how little they seemed in the hole of the mall. She looked at the machinery sitting idly.

They were right.

They should never have left the mall. Lorelei could have gone out to get cheeseburgers until she ran out of money, or just keep maxing out her debit card. Who cared about the service charges or the overdraft fees - her mother would pay for them. In the meantime she was sitting in the middle of a mall half-open to the outside world. A tall sheet of blue board fell near the opening and broke into powdery pieces on the floor near the men.

Sitting in the car a few hundred feet away where the outside of the mall met the remaining inside of the mall, was Carl - the only drive and purpose she could possibly need. He was already notorious in her mind. He was a celebrity. He was every fantasy that encompassed the thick eroticism that bores down through to the white orgasmic center in all of us. The human and her partner. Kink. Reassuring and true. More true than anyone she had ever known. The unconditional truth of a canine. She wondered what she was even still doing in the mall.

She stood and walked toward the door she entered. Out of the corner of her eye she saw the men beginning to disperse as she opened the heavy door and walked down the hallway.

Opening the door to the outside, she saw a tow truck with the front end of her car hoisted in the air as if it was about to take off.

"What the hell are you doing with my car?!"

A small heavy man came around the side of the truck to where she was standing near the back door. He was taking a pair of ratty, stained work gloves off.

- I was told to come tow this for being on private property.

"That is my car! You would just tow it off with my boyfriend in it?"

- What?... I can drop it down so you can get your things out, but I have to take it out of here; that's my orders.

"Get it down, get it down!"

He returned to the control box, and lowered the car down. Her heart burned, anticipating seeing him again, even in the moments to come. The sometimes, the empty times, the times apart; Carl rendered these inconsequential. The car was inconsequential. Everything in it was meaningless. But him. Moments of life were nothing when they couldn't see one another. They weren't the paintings that were mass produced, caked with color, hanging from the walls of a pediatrician's office. They were color itself...

As the car came to eye level, Lorelei saw Carl sitting in the passenger seat, slumped over. Lorelei thought about Carl playing like a toy for a situation such as this - he was motionless. He was ingenious. She needed to see his eyes. His smile. His reassurance. She needed to taste his kiss.

"Could you please give me a couple minutes... I am not stealing the car or anything, I just need some... privacy." She gave him the look that you give men saving them the embarrassment of witnessing the unloading of thirty boxes of tampons from the back seat. It works in times like these.

- Hurry up.

He slowly turned, opened the cab to his tow truck, and got in.

She opened the passenger door. Heat poured from the cabin.

"Psst!"

Nothing.

Lorelei felt something, though. A precognitive feeling. Hunched over in the car, he was motionless. Her burning heart cindered, and molten lead dripped down to her stomach. She knew something, but didn't recognize it right away. Or didn't want to. The recognition bubbled up, and she suppressed it. It is easier to be absent minded now. She walked to the passenger side of the car and opened the door.

"Psst!"

He was still hunched over in the seat. She seemed to know before she even left the car that she would be witnessing this right now. She thought back to his voice. No, no no no no, no. So rotten. He rolled the windows up. So deep and so rotten was the pain that was washing over her.

"No!" she managed to order out. She half expected him to move and indicate he was still pretending. "NO!" she forcefully replied to herself, and shoved his shoulder lightly. How selfish could he be? Really. This was so lowly. So sharp. So horribly painful. She swooned and was apprehensive, nauseous and insane. Only his body remained. No animation. Nothing.

She stormed back to the other side of the car, opened the driver's door, and got in. The windows were still rolled up, and noxious fumes of contracted burnt plastic began to suffocate her. She looked at the tortured, motionless corpse of her most loved and was dizzied by the gases and the heat. She locked her door. She locked whatever doors remained to be locked.

She wrapped one hand around her lover, and with the other clawed at the passenger window as she wept. She wept for her ruined love. She wept for her motionless lover with his mouth propped open, and his plastic foam skull contracted and sallow from the heat. She wept for the moments they shared and the memories that remained in her head. She wept.

And she slept. And she felt like she was falling again, but this time it was hot and uncomfortable. When she fell this time, a man was banging on the window of her grisly car and she was sprawled across a center console. And everything was black.

When she awoke later on, she was being strapped into a gurney, and an oxygen mask was being fitted over her mouth. The air in the mask was cold, and she watched the condensation cloud up on the inside of the cup. Turning her head, she watched the tow truck once again lift its fork into the air. Carl's lifeless, hardened, shrunken, withered face fell down into the foot well of the car, unencumbered by her grasp or even the seat belt he had fastened around himself.

The tow truck driver had a black plastic bag in his hand, and he began to stuff empty fast food cups and bags and wrappers from her car into it.

As the brackets of steel and the dusty cinder blocks fell in the background, she wept once more. She wept for her life. She wept for Carl. She wept for the withered, wretched, and wuthering heart that burned in her chest amid such brutality and carnage.

The ambulance began to pull away. Through the back window, she watched as the tow truck driver shoved Carl into the garbage bag, and tossed the bag into the dumpster next to the building.

The backhoe cleared and entire wall away from the building, and Lorelei silently wished that she had met her demise drunk on the fumes of Carl's beautiful, noxious, heartbreaking self.

*Drowning In Bleach While
Everyone Looks On, Astonished*

48

I told my mother-in-law about the wonder of nature's fury, but I neglected to tell her how many times I wished to throw my body into the foamy white rapids while my wife, her daughter, screamed gruesome horror, completely inconsolable by any of the number of strangers suddenly called to duty. They would just see my body leap into the falling water like it was surrounded by smoke, and disappear. It wouldn't even look like I fell. I avoided this while recounting our vacation this year to Niagara Falls to my wife's mother as we drank tea in the living room. I discussed the sight of their magnitude, the tunnels behind them and the rushing water, and the dangerous rapids.

"...it truly was beautiful." The senselessness of this moment was staggering; exhilarating.

"Wow," Jackie responded. Her white hair framed her face softly as she sat on the couch, and she looked at her daughter, surprised at our newest venture out into the wilderness of the world. "I absolutely loved your postcard. It was something - and the one you sent to Charles was very funny. He loves anything in a bikini."

With that the two of them chattered a surprised laugh that cut deep; horrible.

I stood. I couldn't stand it any more.

"Does anyone want any more tea?"

"No, no. Thank you. When is your mother supposed to come over," Katie asked.

"I don't know. Fifteen minutes? I think she was already supposed to be here."

"Oh."

"I am going to go do some things... Could you call me up when she gets here? I am going to go do some things in the shed."

"Sure! We will just be here chatting away."

I walked out the sliding door and into the cool November afternoon. Leaves were scattered over the back yard, and the ones still in the trees danced around in circles on the branches. The wooden rickety door to the shed in the back yard shook as I opened it, and the musty aroma of gasoline and oil wafted out. I pulled the string with the tiny bell on the end, and the florescent light clinked on, electricity bouncing around on the inside of the tube humming dim light into the small room.

On the small workbench lay a pipe, sawdust and a worn out patch of wood, an old screwdriver that was dad's, and an empty Budweiser can that had ashes in it. I slid the can of tobacco over to the edge of the workbench and removed a pinch of tobacco, tapped the pipe on the old beer can, and stuffed it. Lighting the pipe wafted chords of aromatics into the enclosed shed, the same aromatics that bled into the wooden walls and worn boards of the floor which mixed with oil and gasoline to create its comforting milky tan atmosphere.

There were so many opportunities for the light of myself to become apparent. I wanted to become a carpenter of fine furniture, but instead worked thirty years at a construction company under the iron fist of the overbearing wife who only focused on buying things for the family that would go bad. Get broken. Disappear when the kids were teenagers. Not matter. It was all shit. What we needed was a nice boat. A workshop for the rustic unfinished chairs I was going to make. Everything else and everything but what we have.

The small measure of comfort was in this wooden shed with the radio that still got the classical station I liked and lasted a good twenty years. It was all an experiment, this life. An experiment in clean living and family connoisseurship. Thirty three years of marriage and two dogs and three children who were doted on by Katie and who I hardly knew. Now they are off doing whatever at their colleges. I don't even know their phone numbers. I don't even know them, because they were Katie's.

Outside, I heard that she let the dog out on the lead, and he began barking. She named him Babbages. Even the dog was hers. Everyday, the eighty pound dog had the same routine. It woke. It went outside. It barked at the same spot in the backyard. It would not stop barking until one of us went outside and reeled him in on his wire runner like a fish. It was inconsolable until it was pulled up to the back door by its collar, and pointed toward the door. It then bounded into the kitchen, ran to the food bowl, knocked it and his water across the floor, and then ate up the sloppy mess like he was fulfilling a scavenger hunt. This was repeated throughout the day three times until it was bedtime. He was an absolute wreck. A mama's boy. A very bad dog.

I picked up the screwdriver with the wooden handle and scraped it across the divot I created in the wood. Sooner or later I will have bored a line into the workbench that is so deep it will not be able to support its weight anymore. The line looked like the scraggly horseback riding trails in the desert atmosphere of Arizona when we were on vacation there. The one thing that Katie afforded me was the opportunity to take yearly vacations with her and leave the kids at home.

But I would always fantasize about killing myself in various ways while she reacted with astonished terror at the senselessness of it.

When we were in Arizona I thought about getting off of my horse to pee beside the trail while the guide and the others went ahead to give me privacy. Then I would put a rock in the horse's anus, or pee on it, or something, and get it to kick me in the head. Or lay down so it would step on me. Something violent and awful. There was an old cemetery near my parent's house growing up in New England where all of the markers described the buried as being kicked by a horse or struck by lightening or dying as an infant. Something like that would be great, but there was no romance in it. It would have looked like an accident.

It only took a moment before Babbages began barking, and my smoke and solace was interrupted because it was certainly my responsibility to take care of him. I was his concierge when Katie had put him outside. He was my responsibility when she had done her part and I was enjoying some down time. Everything was my responsibility when it was timed correctly to intersect with my freedom and extra time. I tapped out the tobacco cinders, left the shed, grabbed the beast by the collar, dragged him onto the porch, pointed him in, and released his runner. He bounded around the corner. A splash, a rustle, and sloppy sounds emanated from his corner of the kitchen. I followed him in.

After the horseback ride, we went on a walk around a horseshoe shaped platform above the Grand Canyon. Eighty-five dollars. Each. Invigorating. I thought of throwing myself off of the side, but it would have been too difficult to make it look intentional, or be kept from doing it if I were to make it look intentional. Too little.

"I am going to do it," I said aloud, softly. The dog took no notice. He was making a mess with the bowl. Cinnamon and apples were in the air because of a candle Katie had lit while I was outside. The candle had two wicks in a soup of wax, and had a picture of apples on a sticker on the front. This was the new state of things - the candle looked like what it was. Like what space food pills represented in old science fiction movies. This was the apple pie that my wife made me. The apple pie of the future.

The flame flickered and reminded me of the vacation in Manhattan. I had taken my Zippo with me and planned out that we were going on a walk and I was going to cover a set of long underwear in Sterno and wear them under my clothes and set myself on fire while we walked in Central Park. One minute we're walking, and the next, combustion. A romantic idea, but in hindsight not at all practical.

I was preparing in the bathroom of the hotel after my shower. I removed the long underwear from the packaging, opened the Sterno with the lid of my lighter, and emptied the contents into the sink. I had thought there would be a great deal more fuel in the three cans of it I had brought, and then thought about the concept of it... The Sterno doesn't burn, the gas does. But maybe it would make a big impact on my clothes - Sterno soaking through them. Probably burn my skin and begin to smell before I ever got to the park after dinner. What was I thinking? Katie began knocking on the door frantically because she wanted to know what I was doing, and there I was with long underwear wrappers all over the bathroom, a sink with a little Sterno in it, my suit still on a hanger, and I wasn't even dried off from my shower yet.

It was a disaster. I had to wash the fuel down the sink, I threw the long underwear away because it was August, and let her use the toilet while I dressed in the cold hotel room which she had air conditioned to the point where we could store meats from hooks in it. A ridiculous plan. Poorly executed. The new plan would be gasoline in zipper bags that I store under my clothes inconspicuously.

The doorbell to the house rang. It was my mother. She stormed in, her blond hair waving wispy in the air while she gave me a quick half-kiss, and carried herself straight into the living room as I followed close behind her. The wet kiss on my cheek evaporated coolly as she addressed the other women in the room.

"Ruth! Ruth, Ruth, Ruth! How are you!" The three cackled and sputtered in hard and cantankerous jest. Ruth was my mother's name, and every time she saw my wife, she addressed her as such. By her own name. I looked at my wife, and whispered 'I am really going to do it,' but no one noticed. No one even paid any attention at all. There was nothing complete about this and we were all coming from something so very, so very dull and haphazard. They were finished hugging.

"Yes, Ruth, how are you?" her mother responded. Was this a cadence? A bizarre social call and response? They did this sick, sick, twisted, sick boring, banal performance every time they were together; on and on and on.

"Give me everything, I am so unique!" Katie responded.

"You are, you are!" My mother replied.

"Honey, would you put more tea on?" Katie asked.

"I am..."

And I turned to the kitchen and put the kettle back on. I could kill them with some bleach, I suppose. I could slip some apple juice and bleach in the tea and tell them it was fucking apple tea. Tell them it was delicious. Tell them that it would soon be midnight and narcissism all together no matter what was happening to them as they drifted off to sleep. Or threw up. This wouldn't work.

The rain-sound of the beginning of boiling water began, and I looked under the sink for the bleach. If I did this right I could put the bleach in a shallow pan, lay in it, and take one triumphant breath in and drown haphazardly in two inches of chlorine in a five quart casserole dish. If I was determined enough, I could do this. I could be drowning in bleach while everyone looked on astonished as the teakettle whistled in the background. And they would all laugh because they didn't believe it had just happened. They would think it was a joke. They wouldn't even know what the hell they were looking at. And as the chlorine destroyed my lungs and ate through my nasal passages, my wife would poke me laughing, and scream blood in a feverish pitch when she realized I wasn't getting up. This would be the beginning of my joyful accomplishment.

The kettle whistled, and I brought it into the living room with fresh teabags.

"Honey, would you bring us some more lemon and milk," Katie asked as I poured the hot water into their waiting cups. I turned back into the kitchen, replaced the kettle on the stove, took the bleach out from under the sink, twisted the cap off, and smelled the opening. The acidity, or the palish sulfuric smell, or I wouldn't know how to describe it. I then covered it again and replaced it below the sink. White specks of chlorine dust were on my fingers. I wiped them onto a towel, and then took a lemon from the fridge and cut it on the cutting board. I grabbed the milk. I smiled again as I brought it into the living room. I poured the milk into the small pourer and placed the lemons on the plate of lemons.

"Honey, do stay and have a seat."

"I have to put the milk back."

"Yes, but come back," I put the milk back and returned. "It really was nice of you to come all this way, Ruth, all joking aside."

"Oh, thank you. I have to come see my son and my daughter in law once in a while," my mother replied. "I am so happy to see that you are getting on without the kids around. I can't believe that Stanley has finally moved off to college. He and his brothers are off being adults, and you are finally here alone in your own little nest. How has it been?"

"Oh, wonderful. I still feel like the kids that bought this place twenty five years ago, I really do-"

"-Oh, I remember that," her mother chimed in laughing, "you were both so very happy when you came here - do you remember that?"

"We do, we do," she responded looking at me, "it is like we have had our family this whole time, dreaming of a time that we wouldn't be worried anymore about them and be able to be together with just ourselves... It is wonderful. It is just wonderful."

"I am so happy for you two, Ruth - " her mother stopped, interrupting herself at mistakenly calling her own daughter by her mother-in-law's name. They laughed. "No, I mean Katie. It must be really nice, to get to know each other again and everything."

"Oh, thank you mom," Katie said, brushing lint off of her knee and taking a sip of tea.

"So," my mother began with a smirk, "how is the sex? Isn't it better after menopause? You don't have to worry about anything!

It is so natural and fun!" All of the women laughed. I am really going to do it. I rubbed the back of my hand with my thumb. "I can remember after that I felt like crap for a year, but I was after everything after that. I was buying all sorts of things on the Internet and," and I stopped listening.

My wife and her mother were looking back and forth at each other, surprised at the starkness of my mother's discussions which always inevitably turned to sex. I can't remember the last time we had sex. She would lie to my mother and to friends about an experimental, tantric, erotic, and sensual sex life that they all yearned for. The longer time went on, the more stories of bedroom adventure, the more deep and intense the descriptions of our animal magnetism, the less we became intimate. The less we would know each other. I satisfied her hunger for comfort every night, and she covered our sex life verbally with her friends, satisfying what she possibly thought was her obligation to me every day.

It was terrible.

"I am going to do it," I whispered. My mother was still going on about the joys of post-menopausal sex. My wife humored her with stories that weren't true about our relationship. Or maybe she believed them. I couldn't listen.

"I am going out," I said aloud, cutting my mother off. They all looked at me.

"O...K..." Katie replied. "If you are going to pick something up, could you stop by the supermarket while you are out? You know, your mother drove all this way, and it would be-"

I left the room, and walked up to our bedroom, grabbed my keys, got in the car, and left. I didn't take the list, because I wasn't going to go to the supermarket. I was thinking of going to the library, or maybe the liquor store to get a beer and drink it in the car. There was nothing to do now that I was out. I should have brought my pipe and bought some weed or something.

But I wouldn't know where to buy it. This wasn't thirty years ago and I wasn't a freshman in college. I was a family man. I was timid and spreading my expertise among no one but a family of books in my small library in the living room. *Swann's Way, Vanity Fair*, the *Frost Reader, Paradise Lost*, they sat watching me on my way through the daily mundanes of retirement. Originally I thought it would be a welcome respite - this short vacation of the rest of my life. My hands pointing toward the heavens of the rest of my life. But this completeness, a virtuous yet boring broken fortune of time has left me with only those stacks of friends. They lay, well worn and digested many times, the middles black with many thumbings and readings.

These days there was an honest emptiness in the daily routine, though. It didn't seem like Katie and I knew one another, and it didn't appear that we ever did. It seems that we had an honest and wonderful five years at the beginning of our relationship, but that statement may be an arrogant over-assumption these years later. We didn't know each other. I knew how to make her happy - it was easy. Be in bed by 9:30 every night. Spoon. Nuzzle. Have breakfast and coffee ready with the paper in the morning. Be warm. Comfort. Slow, sensual talk. Embrace. The arching goodness of an abstract life of consumption.

But she never had any idea that I wanted at least one swift fucking every evening. That a birthday present needn't be a tie or a tool or anything but a humble curdling scream while we made love. My name. Anything. If I had been a particularly good husband, an outfit. She could dress as a frau I met at Oktoberfest two years ago, or a Victorian woman of affluence, or a school girl. Once or twice, she could have invited a nameless thin friend from her quilting group, or walked into our bedroom completely naked with an old flame of mine. Or a friend intent on making love for the rest of the night. Something but the silent, boorish, and paper-worky sex that we have engaged ourselves with the entire marriage.

It was this that I reflected upon parked outside of Senses Adult Boutique two towns over. The ramshackle building with curling white paint flaking off was seemingly the only place I could think of coming to on a day such as this - one when I escaped a den of musky estrogen.

I walked in to the store. A young man with a goatee was at the counter, fully engaged at something on the computer. He was thin, and his shirt hung off of his body as if there were only a skeleton painted with flesh and wispy black hair.

"Good afternoon"

"I am really going to do it," I replied. I don't even know why I was doing this. He didn't care.

"If there is anything I can help you find, let me know. Also, if you can't find what you are looking for we can order it and," and somewhere while he was talking I just walked away. I have been unsatisfied with the level of customer service that I have been receiving lately wherever I go, that is, unsatisfied because there has been too much and I am paid attention to. I think a new mission would be to do it. It will be to do it in front of Katie and a salesperson when they are badgering me. I will do it by biting an electric cord, and Katie will lose it, and the salesperson would have to live with it the rest of their life, too, having seen this horrifying image of a man testing the resilience of the appliances he sells with his mouth.

The store was horrific and neon. It was an apparition, filled with bright lights and fluorescent colors. Why was it that these fluorescent dreams were what fueled the fantastic sexual fantasies of men? Was it the excitement of color? The attraction of the electric? Was this the same theory behind the loud and masochistic florescence of sports car's Pantone offerings? Did any thought even go into it? Was it just coincidental that everyone had the same ideas? And why did the Chinese buffets in town border their windows with the same neon lights?

I went up and down the aisles, taking in the magazines, films, toys; purchases that would otherwise have a brilliant and stark effect on my wife's conceptualization of the core of my being. It was a simple decision. I would buy as much as I could, and treat myself to one particular big purchase, the sexualized object in rubber, and one that would utterly prove the particulate being with the four chambered heart and high metabolism rate, my wife, completely useless once and for all.

I went to the front of the store and took a handbasket. I filled it with various magazines with hardly clothed and stark naked girls on the covers. My ancient fingertips slipped across the glossy covers as I tossed the young ladies into my basket, ignoring the consuming aspect of it for now to pretend these photos, these collections, these blatant and stylized embracing youth were sending me their photos personally... Or that I was there with them. There is nothing to remember but the wonderful beauty that I missed so many years ago. I could have really scored with them had I the opportunity years ago. There is virtually no time to think about the very real time wasted.

I embraced the ones with the teenie girls pretending they are younger than they really were, the magazines with them on top of one another, licking, kissing, embracing one another. On top of one another. It was a game. And I avoid the others, primarily the ones with these same girls of the industry sitting on their rears, naked, poised to receive all sorts of fluids on their faces with their mouths agape. There was no romance in it, not in addressing it as an industry. Industry of flesh and corpulent sweat and sticky movement. No romance in it at all. The better ones were the young ones by themselves, smelling of soaps and drugstore spray perfume.

My gaze was pulled to the the wall of toys. Some for women, and then others for men. It was the ones for men that I was interested in. I had gotten a catalog in the mail once a month or so advertising marital aids that feature the heavily made up model's face caked with eyeliner and spray can tan. They would be advertising a particular massager as they called it. It was always a personal men's massager, modeled after the model's own parts.

There was nothing in the catalog that described it or showed the product except for the model, her face washed with an ecstasy that looked as though they had cut her hand while they were taking the picture so that only the crew saw the pain she was in but shoppers could see the ecstasy that was pumping through her blood and her velvety core at that very moment. And that is what this all was; life. This life was before I met Katie, and now my jungle instincts and passionate heart has all but dissolved through my rotting ribcage.

I walked up to the wall and carefully selected a box. Shining in the light, my face reflected through the polyurethane plastic bubble package. On the front, a sensuous woman dressed as a hussy. This wasn't her, what was in this package. That would be filthy. Industry. I turned the box over and could see a fleshy tube in the form of a vagina. This was unacceptable. It was horrific. It was purple. I put it back. The wall was carpeted in these boxes, cold and unwelcome. The racks at the end, however, with their insulating cardboard called me over to their seamless, inarticulate, sensuous packaging.

There was only one that I needed. I am really going to do it.

The box stared at me. There was a woman on the front posed in inky splendor, her ass raised in the air, her head peeking from behind one of her knees. Her face didn't matter. It was her product that did. The box read "Robin Foster's Real Pussy and Ass." It was glossy and primeval. It was the epitome of the guise that was so missing. This body, soulless and devoid of anything that would be reminiscent of a woman. It was the product that mattered. I turned the package over. Behind a plastic window, sitting on a throne of cardboard, was the round rump of a human ass, the puckered eye of an anus, and a beautiful and shapely smooth vulva. There was even the beginnings of a pair of legs, but cut off before they could be too much of a nuisance. This was a find. The price tag read $239. It was worth it.

I brought it to the front counter.

"Did you find everything you were looking for?"

"I did. Thank you."

He rang up the merchandise quickly and it appeared that my stock in this business was growing exponentially.

"Can I interest you in a membership in the -"

"No."

"But you will save $25 today, even with the membership costs."

"I am really going to do it!"

"So you would like me to sign you up?"

"No!" He paused, confused, and put my merchandise into the black plastic shopping bags.

"Your total is $439.60..." I handed him my card. "Credit?" He swiped it, I signed my receipt, and I left.

I put the bags in the back seat of the car, and took the Real Pussy and Ass from its bag. This was an amazing new experience. A rush. A fulfillment of things that I was so sorely lacking in my world and my masculine needs. I was going to put Robin Foster's Real Pussy and Ass in my shed, and I will have something new to scrape. This would be a beautiful and magnificent moment. A new era of retirement.

The car rustled on, and I pulled the shifter out of park and drove it onto the thoroughfare. It was getting dark out, and the lights of the businesses along the streets had clicked on.

Fall was an absolutely bizarre season, and as it came to a close, the darkness soaked the world in a dim haze at odd, early hours. It couldn't have been four-thirty yet, but headlights beamed in and the store's signs up and down the street pulled your eyes shut with the glare and unpleasantness as it is contrasted with dusk. You didn't know whether to put your sunglasses on or the visor down or just squint. It is a mess.

I drove right onto Elizabeth Avenue and a left onto Forest Street, and it got darker and darker. I was sure that the women at home were chatting about how my wife's name was my mother's name over and over again so much that they didn't even realize that I wasn't home yet. It would blend in to a noisy chicken shack. This night would be a lonely orgy in the shed in the backyard, where I could be alone with my lesbians and my Teflon gel molded vagina and be alone. All night. Drunk.

I pulled into the parking lot of the liquor store and bought three bottles of Cabernet and a large bottle of Heineken, and back into the car. There was no time. I was carrying special cargo. Sharp right out of the lot, onto main, and toward home.

This was a special night of passion and romance.

And then the siren and the lights dampened the mirrors and the back window. This was a special night of passion and romance and this had no purpose.

A dark figure approached the window, and I rolled it down.

"Can I see your license and registration, please?" I flushered through the glove compartment, retrieved the tattered paper, and handed it to him with my license. "Do you know why I pulled you over?"

"No officer."

"Okay." He turned and made his way back to the cruiser. His lights were still on, blaring through every visible reticule of free space devoid of light. My eyes couldn't take it. They were shaking.

As time crawled, I had nothing to think about except the hours of time that I am missing out on beginning that very moment. That night was a splendid, and this was something I could not manage to wrap my mind around. This was something that my mind couldn't execute at all. Here he was, in his car, pulling this man over for who knows what reason, badgering his completely clean traffic record to death. What does it take to make this happen any sooner? There was nothing. This is nonsense.

I begged that someone come save me, and I begged it often. This was no different, and all I could do was breathe and wait. Fresh air that smelled like wet granite wrapped around my heart and soaked it in its heaviness. I looked in the back seat at the paper bag from the package store. Welcoming and brief, it wanted to be taken that moment, but I was grateful that I didn't have the beer in the parking lot. This was ridiculous.

Time floated away, and Katie was probably laughing at my eccentricities with our mothers. There was nothing that was redeeming about being alone together. They were the trifecta of grief to anyone that stood in the middle of their conversation at any given moment. They were goddesses of gab, and nothing was too easy a target... There were only two things that would shut her up forever, and one was if she died.

"Step out of the car, please... Put your hands on the vehicle." Just as he was saying this, he took my hands and gently placed handcuffs on them. "You have the right to remain silent. Anything you say -"

"Hi, excuse me." He stopped. I looked into the car's backseat. There were black bags, a brown paper bag, and a blatantly obscene piece of rubber behind a cellophane window in a cardboard box. "Before you tell me what my rights are, could you please tell me what crime I have committed? Why I was pulled over? What I did?"

"I pulled you over because I could see from my cruiser that your registration sticker on your license plate was expired - it is from February two years ago. Then I ran your plates and license and it turns out that you also have a license that has been expired for three years."

"But my wife is in charge of-"

"It doesn't matter, sir,

"How was I supposed to know that it was expired?"

"If we are going to have this conversation, I have to warn you that you have the right to remain silent, and anything you say or do from this point on can be used in a court of law. You can speak with a lawyer, and if you can't afford a lawyer one will be provided to you, do you understand?"

"Yes."

"Good. We are going to impound your car and take you to the station. I am going to book you for driving with an expired license and registration, and then you can call your wife to come and get you and post bail. The whole thing won't take very long, and you will have your car and everything back by the end of the night. These are all misdemeanors and it will probably cost you a lot of money, and if I can just suggest something to you, I would not say too much until you can get a traffic lawyer into the station. Between you and I these things are pretty easy to clear up. But this is just my opinion."

I wanted to tell him to fuck his opinion. I wanted to tell him how very badly I needed to get home. I needed to see my wife, and be home with my mother. Mothers. The mothers.

"I understand, officer. Is there any way to accomplish this without having to call my wife. Could we take care of this here?"

"You don't have a license. You could post bail and take a bus home, but we would still have your car and everything."

"Yeah... You are right."

The officer walked me to the back of the cruiser and had me sit in the back seat. It was cold and unfortunate. Two more cruisers came up behind the one I was in and put their lights on. I heard an echo of strings; an orchestra of strings in my ears as I watched the blues and yellows and whites dance and sparkle on the dew and dirt in the back window. It refracted kaleidoscopic on the roof of the cruiser and was mellowing and quiet. My concentration was occasionally broken by a passing car or truck, the passengers gaping wide-eyed at the scene. They looked into my eyes as if I were a hardened criminal shoved into the back of a police car for distributing drugs to elementary school children, or cutting up the body of a prostitute and distributing her body parts across town like Johnny Appleseed. A piece here, a bit there.

The final thought was more probable as the cars drove by and the officers searched the black bags in my back seat. They removed the molded pussy and ass from the wrapper and the plastic bag, holding it up and laughing at the spectacle they couldn't believe they were witnessing. Horrific faces peered from the slowly passing traffic, and some mothers were reaching in the back seat and covering their children's eyes. Some obviously thought it was an actual body part (albeit from any angle it was difficult to tell what they were looking at but a jiggly lump of flesh devoid of any gore). The spectacle was unique. Some passing men embarrassingly knew exactly what they were looking at.

This was unprofessional. This was a travesty. I wanted to be home.

Two hours later, they were finished tearing my car apart. From where I sat watching, it was obvious that there were masturbators and pornographic magazines strewn all over the inside of my car. The officer returned as the car was being towed. He was silent, and was obviously uncomfortable with his situation.

Being the chauffeur of the man whose backseat was filled with a night of pornographic debauchery. This was an embarrassment. I needed to speak in generalizations.

"What happens with people who leave their cars in impound?"

"They just stay there."

"So, if someone wanted to leave it there and wait until they could drive again, there wouldn't be any issues?"

"I think they charge you for using the space after a certain time, but I am not the person to ask about that."

"Thanks."

"No problem."

When we arrived at the police station, I was booked, my photo was taken, and they fingerprinted me. A man that looked like a bulldog led me down a cinder block hallway with thick off-white paint. He was fat, muscular, and wide.

"You have a phone call," he said in front of a low bank of phones. I thought for a moment, and was not sure if I wanted to use the phone. I needed more time to think.

"Do I need to make it now," I asked.

"I will see what I can do," he replied, and led me down the hallway to the holding cells. There was no one in them, and I was put into one by myself. "Did you eat dinner yet?"

"No."

"I will see what I can do," and just like that, he left.

I walked to the bench in the corner of the room, and sat. There was just a bench. That was all there was. I missed my wife, and I missed my mother. I missed the warmth of our house, and the ease of living. I missed the banter of her mother, and the fun in the old inside jokes that they had. There was nothing that I particularly needed to be upset about, or even annoyed. This was the very top of what every family should be completely driven to accomplish. This was accomplishment, and I mixed it up in just one stupid mistake.

These police officers with their smugness and their desire to accomplish living their lives. There was nothing but an existence in their purpose. To keep the world safe for their daughters to go to school confidently and serenely. To protect. To serve. Their life's one purpose was to allow life to exist, plainly. This was all and existential abyss, in a sense. I was receiving the maximum penalty - the bizarre and strange betrayal of the sexual necessities of man. This is where I messed up. I am a strange fetish.

I have no friends, no girlfriends or sons that would make this as painless as possible. No daughters whom I have had to keep my own secrets with. There was nothing that would make this any easier on Katie. This was a complete mess.

The walls were ashy and caked thick with paint, and there was nothing to do but sit. I had thought about how wonderful it would be to be in solitary confinement in a prison, allowed to read, eat, write letters and keep in touch with the outside world. The stigma with prison was that there was nothing but criminals in it. All of that space that could be used for reclusive artists who need to eat and live was completely wasted on the lawless. People more lawless than I was. That said, there was nothing to tell me what exactly would happen if I just sat here and never posted bail... Would I be in this cell forever?

An hour and a half later, an officer brought me a a piece of fried chicken and a biscuit. It was greasy and delicious. My heart probably couldn't handle it. Four hours and thirty seven minutes later, my mother bailed me out. I told her that I would pay her back the cash that she spent on my release. I was given my wallet, belt, keys, and the big, black plastic bag at the window before we left.

She drove me home, silently. There was peace in the isolation. I seemed to know what was good for me now - this solitary confinement and stark blankness in the isolation. It was beautiful. What I didn't know was how I was going to accomplish this in my daily life. This was good for me. I did what I could for her.

It was slightly apparent now why I wanted to bury secrets into my blatant and violent demise in front of her. It was the ultimate in complicating confusion. It would have been an ocean of red, red, red curdling meaninglessness. That is where the horror would have been. The senselessness. The blackness. The void.

We pulled up the driveway, and my mother pulled herself out of the car slowly, as did I. I held her arm, and we walked up the steps and into the front door. Behind it was Katie with her hand on her forehead, and her mother's arm around her. They shuffled ever so close, and slowly wrapped their arms around me. Her mother did, and she did, and my mother did, and they softly breathed in my ear.

Katie began weeping, and I couldn't understand what was happening.

"Don't... Don't ever leave me again," Katie said, "I can't bear

to think that you were missing, and gone, and not here anymore."
And she began crying. Our mothers moved into the other room,
and she locked her hands around my neck so she could see my face,
and seemed to hang off of me.

This tragic, hopeless, and awful sight was horrible. I
couldn't bear it, and I began to feel upset; like tar was pored into my
chest. I cried. I cried from the depths of my heart, and we both
swayed and cried, and the floor creaked below us, and our hearts
beat slower and heavier than they ever had before.

"I couldn't even guess where you were..." she continued. "I
couldn't bear it. Why didn't you call?"

"Because, I really couldn't imagine what I should do at all," I
managed, "I couldn't think."

"I feel like I got you back; you are so important to me. All I
could think about was having to be here on my own, all of the
time."

That is something I couldn't think about. I couldn't think
about her trying to manage, and what she was going to do when her
mother died, and what she would do when my mother died, and as
everyone in our lives actually began to disappear and vanish,
leaving only us. It was only us, and there was nothing solitary
about it. We have existed for so long. We have existed in our
habitat and made an effort to keep our gutters and our minds clean,
and this effort was why there was nothing so wrong with anything.
The amazing aspect of our lives has been that we have managed to
live them so wonderfully for so long.

And we would both remain watching the falls. We would
both remain in the hot air balloon basket. We would both shop for
appliances and leave alive. We would remain a permanent fixture

in the world and in our home. The spectacle of my existence would remain to be that I managed to exert a great deal of dignity in our final years.

"You are all I have left," I told her. There was nothing new, and everything is old, and we didn't spread each other too thin, and we make each other manic, and there is something that can be said for people that stay exactly the same.

"Be kind to me, and never leave the house." She laughed, softly. "I can only deal with one of these disasters a lifetime, and at your mother's age there is no excuse."

"I couldn't help it."

"I know. Just be kind to me." She wiped her tears from her face with her hand. "Tell me you love me every day, and be kind and be here. I want to be here with you, and this is our journey. The road has been long, and hard at times, but let's make the most of what we have left just now."

Katie pulled my hand, and we walked past the electric carving knife in the cabinet, and the bleach under the sink, and the electrical sockets, and every other deadly element in our home, as if they weren't there at all. It seemed to work finally, and everything was steady and pure, and I unpacked my heart on the sofa. We continued to look at the vacation photos, and the familiarity of the moment, and the level steadiness of my mother's hands and Katie's love didn't seem to be there before. But somehow, they were there now.

October Allows
The Loneliest Days

74

Emilene was dead long before the paper arrived that day. Long before it was printed, long before Harold picked it up with jittery hands and shuffled it into the kitchen, and long before he even considered the thought. It only crossed his mind as he steadied his sixty-four year old hand over the crossword puzzle convulsing out the word pestilence; a ten letter word for "venomous, fatal affliction."

He looked up from the inky mess, reflecting on the last time he heard her voice. It was months ago, and yet he wasn't inspired to call... He only leafed to the obituaries and the odor of the cold, wintry, fresh ink washed over his nose from her name. Emilene Holmes. She kept Harold's name despite her new marriage, and his heart burned molten over the rest of the sentence, "loving mother and wife left behind her husband Rock and daughter Margaret."

He read the sentence fruitlessly several times over. It was as if she were leaving behind only a man whose namesake bore no resemblance to dead Hollywood actors of demure quality, and a daughter who would love her more than anything this cruel world could provide. Yet this same cruel world provided no mention of Harold, a man that would discover he loved her more than the spans of heaven and the beauty of Eden. Harold could only speculate that he would make it to the gates of paradise to even see Emilene again.

"How is the portfolio business treating you, Harold?" Rock asked after mass. Regardless of the divorce, they still attended the same church.

"Well, very fine indeed..." although certain politicians were causing the market to dramatically digest one's nest egg like a serpent. "Your practice?"

"Couldn't be better! I am actually helping Margaret with her college bills... I really wish you would too. A custom investment portfolio would assist her quite nicely." Harold envisioned reaching for his jaw as if he were to surprise him with a kiss and then tearing at his neck flesh with his teeth like a reptile. Emilene politely stared at him, her pale blue eyes mercurially elevating Harold's spirits enough for a pleasant transaction.

"How are you, Harold?" ever so softly.

"Okay, I suppose..." Harold responded, his bobbing, shaking head nullifying his masculinity, "very well, thank you." She just stared at him. A quick, pert, meaningless smile crossed her face, right before she and Rock turned to leave. Yes, it was a pleasant transaction; a pleasant transaction at the bank.

Harold last spoke with her on the phone the last day he was allowed to call. Rock had instructed her that she wasn't to talk to Harold without him present, as the pair of them were too prone to "emotionally unstable outbursts," as he put it. She had told him how she was doing, how the house was, the inane activities of her new cat, and the last time she had spoken with their daughter.

Harold began his side of the conversation with an embarrassing venture into why he missed Emilene, when would he see her, and how very much he loved her, although he wished he never did. They would weep at each other, making it impossible to solve anything. After every conversation, they were reminded of Emilene's great mortal tragedy; the rotten cancerous onion munching at her side. He pleaded to Emilene as he could to stay with him, return and forget his misgivings, but she wouldn't.

After a lengthy discussion on the eve of their thirty-second wedding anniversary, Harold decided that he had a simple decision to make. As nothing more than a compulsive introvert, it was time for him to move out. He liked being alone, and with a new apartment downtown he would be afforded the luxury of solitude for the first time in decades.

Through a muffle of tears, Emilene mustered, "when can I visit, then?"

"No."

"When will I see you, husband? My love?"

"No."

They didn't speak, but after his liquor store excursions, Harold would often find aromatic pink envelopes on the doorstep addressed to him in cursive. But he wouldn't open them, rather, he lined them up on the kitchen counter to serve as decorative coasters for the ever-growing chorus line of empty square whiskey bottles chronicling his historic months of sloth and depravity. But he was perfectly happy being utterly depressed and heartbroken.

It wasn't until years after the undemanding divorce that he had found out about his wife's marriage to a prominent doctor of otolaryngology practicing in Boston. It was that day that he remembered she was missing, and that he loved her. He was then willing to give her anything, and in one cold late-October evening was almost struck down by a car as he shouted, "You are so pretty, here is my blood! You are so lovely! Here are my bones! I miss your heart and flesh!" He realized after dodging the rusty clunker that neither the doctor nor his new wife were at home at all.

As the weeks and months passed, Harold missed Emilene exponentially, and after talking to her a week after she hung up on him sobbing incoherently, he found out about her cancer. No, it seemed there was no time to waste after her diagnosis. Harold called her twice as often, but also called the best hospitals for hours on end, and was unofficially diagnosed as a sociopath by everyone he interacted with.

Recalling his life as he hovered over the early morning paper, he drained his heart and his soul. While a fire in his ribs grew and glassy oil ran from his eyes, he didn't realize that he was sucking on the bitter pulp Emilene's obituary was printed on; he only was aware that October relished in allowing the loneliest days for man, and the expansive drift of Autumn and abandonment existed immortally in life's chaotic spiral.

Fort Point Channels
1995-2009

80

The strength of our memories to create longer, more introspective and powerful versions of events that occurred in our lives has always astounded me – but particularly recently as I stood in line on a rainy Thursday night in a packed hallway. Our circumstance was all the same: we were dressed alike, unfamiliar with one another because of our short, sporadic, and independent approaches we all had toward our personal career advancements. Here we were, 28, 26, 45, 60, all reflecting on our accomplishments, but more about our families waiting for us in the packed auditorium awaiting our appearance and the bestowing of our new credentials and colorful hoods.

I knew my beautiful wife was in the audience, along with my gracious mother, my kind mother in law, and my good friend Jim – all in attendance to support me. But in that hallway it was easy to drift to other things. Tonight would undoubtedly be one of the moments in my life that will continue to reside in my mind for the rest of my life. There have been many others – but only a few stood out as truly magical - abstract-concrete compositions that float around in the warehouse, giant moths in dim light. Silent. Magnificent.

In that hallway of a sea of gowns and unfamiliar faces, I remembered one photograph that I wish I still had that day. One that represents what I remember to be one of the greatest moments of my life.

Imagine a rectangle, the photograph. Awkwardly positioned in the room, the photographer's perspective was slightly askew, taking a position close to the right-hand wall. The floor appears crooked as the camera was snapped haphazardly, and it sits as ragged, listing pock-marked deck beams of a pirate ship. A hundred years of rough dedicated service on the seas of industry. The ceiling opposite the floor was thick posts and beams, industrial, possibly made of the same wood, caked darker with dust or years of neglect. The rear wall in the center was largest at the right, and passed slightly smaller in perspective as the photo travels to the left. It was covered in a colorful urban mural depicting us – we were the inner city buildings and the teenagers that were shown in the picture – youth, baseball caps, colorful baggy clothing, spray-painting productive activism awareness, or at least the semblance of the elements of our identity. A big, block "Studio 10/15," gold and sparkling in the sky.

In front of that wall were the subjects of the photo: I was sitting in the middle of the middle row, surrounded by fifteen or so of my closest friends. Streamers hung from the ceiling, and the smiling faces of these compatriots, these wonderful faces, these family members framed me in a light and an existence that I could never match in my life. This moment in time became one of my most prized possessions in my mind, floating high into the air and barely forgotten, then swiftly down again to remind me that it was still there – that life had not escaped me even when I thought it had.

And that photo eventually disappeared, and only this memory of it remained.

I was here at the college celebrating and creating new memories for myself. The photo was taken fifteen years ago, almost to the day of this graduation. It was May of 1995.

. . .

I waited for that day for a long time. Much like the rest of my life, any semblance of success that was coming in my direction was met in my higher mind by the incredible sinking feeling of tragedy slowly creeping up on me and startling that success; it follows me to this day. Regardless, leading up to this date for the prior four years of my life, I had volunteered my time at this establishment and contributed to its success and its elemental gravity in my home of Boston. This particular May, I turned fourteen years old, and this meant that I was allowed to collect the minimum wage. At that time it was four dollars and twenty five cents an hour at The Children's Museum of Boston, when I was barely more than a child myself.

These years were extremely critical for many reasons. For one, I was coming out of my adolescence and making my way through puberty and trying to make sense of my surroundings. My father had left us when I was nine years old. I would have never become part of my family at the Children's Museum if Dad had not dated the woman who had randomly brought my sister and I there on a school day when I was in the sixth grade. Ironically, it was the closed door of my own blood relations that ultimately opened the door of the surrogate family of lost, disillusioned, and skeptical youth that came together to make something special happen.

At this point, there wasn't really much to find engaging and complete in my life. I felt as though I was falling apart little by little in the small confines of my existence. It even showed as big cherries of painful acne eating away at my countenance. When I was in school, even arriving home was a spectacular engagement. Mother would come home from her job as a vocational teacher at a with a case of Zima. The popular malt beverages would accompany her in the garage alone with a small transistor radio broadcasting talk radio. She would spend her evenings drinking and chain smoking, and occasionally enter the house to eat dinner. She was dealing with her own ghosts at the time, while my sister and I were accompanied by one of her students who had moved in as a result of constant quarrels in her own home.

At times, Mom would routinely display her complete ignorance of what was going on in her children's lives, inappropriately asking questions that even surprised and appalled us. Once, she had asked me, "are you having sex?" Normally this question would evoke shock and a bizarre turn of the stomach coming from your single parent. All I could remember thinking was that I wish that I was, and wondered where she found the fantastical images of the young, nubile, sex-starved ladies I was spending time with to evoke such a question.

"No, Mom." I replied slowly, and with a frustrated level of concern for my sex life just as much as the question.

And we would inevitably be driving when questions like this arose. This particular time it was to the health club my grandmother purchased us a membership for to get us out of the house. Mom would insist that my sister and I go there with her to swim. Grandma insisted we went, so we could get out of the house. She thought mom would be less inclined to drink, she might get herself in shape for a potential suitor, and everything was in the best intentions...

Mom's alcoholism, however, became magically inventive as we drove through the streets and she learned that she could fill travel coffee mugs with a nice cocktail and no one was any the wiser. We rode through her curvy Dr. Seussian Zima roads to the Sheraton's health club, holding our breath the entire ride.

One particular night she was hammered in one of the lounge chairs, and a Hispanic family had begun to come to the club a few weekends earlier. There was a young girl, my age, that was in the family that would make eyes at me while we swam, and she was incredibly beautiful and shy. Mom evidently had been studying us and had seen the same in her. She wanted me to grow a pair of balls, and it was time to have a pep talk with me. Mom to man.

"Go talk to her," she shouted across the indoor pool. Her voice echoed and waved in the air with the scent of chlorine and bleached bath towels. We were the only two families in the Olympic-sized room, and everyone including me certainly heard her. My sister and I, the family, the towel attendant, and the girl. I swam to the side of the pool where she was lounging.

"Mom, I-"

"Go! She's hot! Her nipples are like silver dollars!"

I immediately thought I should invite mom into the pool, in hopes she might dive in somewhere that a head wound wouldn't be unimaginable. Or that I could do the same. Or that I could wait for an answer to any of this that would make sense, and maybe that would. The struggle. The question about whether any of this existence made any sense...

I thought about this over the following weeks; there was something that was much more heroic about suicide when contrasted with being pulled into a drunk driving accident by my alcoholic mother. That there was something heroic about not facing things and continuing to fail and no one to be supportive or even paying attention to me.

I also consciously understood that there was nothing that I could do for myself unless it was in my control. That I truly had to avoid depending on anyone else in order to make it somewhere in this world - with women, with success, with anything. That girl at the pool was completely gorgeous. While my mother probably felt bad about asking me if I was having sex because of her over-protective drunken self, if she remembered it at all, her solution was to hopelessly and offensively try to get me laid. Her intentions were pure.

Needless to say, I made it a point to ensure that I never stepped foot in that heath club ever again. According to my sister who continued to go, that happy Hispanic family with their gorgeous daughter did the same.

So, the museum was respite from a completely dysfunctional aspect of my existence. My family was a combination of all of our lost and troubled souls. Sure, I was extremely lucky – while my story was that my mother was an alcoholic and my dad was gone, some of these kids' parents didn't seem to love them, some didn't have jobs, some couldn't feed them or their siblings. Some were homeless. Some had problems of their own, some by fault of their own and some not. Some had guns, and some needed them. So I banded together with these kids to bring home four dollars and a quarter an hour. To some parents it went to pay rent. To some, groceries. To some, drug habits.

But when we were there, we were more family that a lot of us ever had seen in a long time, and there was definitely something that we all had to offer one another. If there is one major thing that we learned about this experience is an intense revelation of one another, a reevaluation of personal worth and community, a valuation of compassion, and a drive for service.

Compassion, grace, and beauty come most easily to a girl that was arguably one of the most influential people in my life. Karmen Calderon. She was tall. She had short curly hair like shaved dark chocolate that lay on her shoulders, and brown eyes that would go on forever. Her accent was like warm honey on her lips, the words sticky sweet with Latin sound and beauty. She existed in a cloud of sophistication at sixteen, or so it seemed to me at the time as her smile and her silence must have meant nothing less.

I am not entirely sure how it began between us. I was easily intimidated by all young women (or in this case, girls) of my own age, let alone this sixteen year old who was certainly a magnetic figure to me. But there was a strong gravity that developed with no clear origin besides how poorly I felt some days, and she was always there.

I don't remember any of our conversations besides one – but I clearly remember our relationship. The oeuvre of it. It wasn't the creation, but the existence of the body of it. Its spirit. We didn't talk much, and I always felt embarrassed around her. Where everything weighed on my shoulders, the magic of her became so lucid. If I was having an incredibly bad day, she would come and hug me. Her embrace was so pure and exhilarating, her hair smelling of coconut. She would hold my hands. She would look into my eyes and smile. The vividness of this smile, the genuine nature of the smile in her mouth and in her eyes and in the heat of her body. There was a dimple above her top lip. What would it feel like to kiss her? On particularly painful days, she would then lead me somewhere else – somewhere where there would be no museum visitors and no eyes to peer into our hearts. She would sit me down. She would put my head in her lap. She would pat my head. And I never felt safer in my life.

In all of the shocking developments in my life – through mom's alcoholism, her boyfriends, my terrible grades and complete disinterest in school, my inability to create music, bonds, relationships with any of my peers, or catch the eye of any girl my age at all, Karmen's gentle and wordless comfort was one of the most important and amazing things that I have ever experienced. She was a completely pure person. She fulfilled an emptiness and extinguished the pain buried deep within me. Her ability to see right through me, to comfort me for hours with simple human contact, to feel and smell her skin and experience her existence simply became the motivation to continue on with mine.

The day I turned fourteen years old fell on a Tuesday. A huge milestone in my life only because I was now able to earn the Massachusetts minimum wage. Tuesdays were also the days where we would have our weekly staff meetings for the Teen Jobs Program. I took the train to South Station and walked the few blocks to the museum. The smell of Boston went from oily subway, to cigarette smoke, to exhaust, to salt water, to the distinct smell of the museum; a briny antique book scent. My nostalgic Boston was what one would imagine a cartographer's quarters on an ancient ship smelled like: ink, books, lead, liquor. I arrived on time, and I also made sure to bring my birth certificate and social security card to ensure I had everything necessary to fill out my W2 forms and start getting paid.

When I arrived, I met with Deedra, an empowered inspirational woman who was the supervisor of our program. We had our weekly meeting from three-thirty to five that night, as we had every week, and I stayed later to complete the paperwork. I was instructed to take the paperwork to Human Resources to fill it out, which was across the museum on the other side of the historic factory building. The place was empty, save a few people that were straggling in the offices, working ahead to make for an easy Friday. The man who was in charge of the payroll, a tall, thin man with round wire glasses, took my paperwork. As I waited for my copies to be made, Katy, one of the other teens I worked with came and asked me to return to the office because there was a paper I had forgotten.

I got my copies from Human Resources, and I walked with Katy through the exhibits that led to the office back on the other side of the building. She was a skinny, attractive young woman, but her glasses she wore were much too large for her face and it truly made her look ten years older. It wasn't her fault. She was a sweetheart. We passed through an exhibit with a stage and a psychedelic video system that projected your silhouette on the wall in a funky manner, through an exhibit about television complete with a studio and working chroma-key system, an exhibit about teens in Tokyo, and finally we arrived at the giant metal double doors next to the reproduction Tokyo subway car. Katy opened the doors, and the big room was pitch black. It was understanding considering the meeting had finished for the evening and everyone had gone home, but equally vexing because when the lights were off it was impossible to find the switch that was far into the large, black, windowless room.

I turned to her, and she nodded her head indicating that she wanted me to enter and find the switch. She hated the dark, and I studied her face for a lustful gaze thinking she would push me into the room and accost me in the darkness... and while it existed in the wonder of my imagination, not to mention that I had a thing for her in the past, the look was not there. I walked into the room; ten paces, fifteen paces, twenty paces, all the while running my hand along the unfinished wooden sliding door on the right, trying to avoid splinters while also using my memory of the room to find the impossible switch.

The lights flashed on on their own. I felt like I was falling.

"Surprise!" The silence broke from a hundred voices. My eyes adjusted. Daniel was there. And that was Kendric. Jenny. Then Jan, Nikky, and Deedra. Katy came up behind me and hugged me from behind. Lorili. Joanna. Katy let go. There were even more people, and around everyone hung streamers. Balloons. Glitter. Decoration.

The bland room was transformed into life. Pizza lay on a table with soda, cake. Someone turned music on, and everything was symphonics, smiles, voices, and love. My heart beat in my chest in amazement, and in my ears in astonishment. My eyes studied my surroundings. It was uncanny.

Then silence. My eyes stopped. In the midst of the bodies, the streamers, the movement, there was a face that radiated above all others.

Karmen stood smiling, silently; modestly. She slowly made her way through everyone. Methodically weaving through the confusion, she looked like the ideal specimen, an animal, perfect and sanguine. It would be cliché to mention she looked like a lioness, but there was something primal about what I was seeing, and I wished I could see it happen over the decades. I wished she was naked, only so I could study the beauty and mechanics of her body...her muscles as she moved. And she arrived just as slowly. And she put her arms around me just as slowly. And I breathed in her scent, and she kissed me on the cheek, and the bustle started up again.

I immediately got hugs from all directions. This was my family. This was my family celebrating my birthday. I trembled with self betrayal. I trembled, and I thought I didn't deserve any of this.

For the rest of my life I battled these same feelings. What did I deserve? I didn't deserve anything. These feelings of worthlessness may be the source of the manifestation of my anxieties as they build up whenever a big event nears and I am awarded some sort of recognition. I have made it, or I have worked hard for it, and I do not deserve it whatsoever.

Regardless, we ate pizza, talked, and celebrated me. Everyone had something to say. A hat made of recycled tubes leftover from some manufacturing process was bestowed upon my head. I was presented a giant greeting card that everyone in the building had signed. I was also presented with a giant paycheck that looked just like the paychecks everyone on the museum's regular payroll got for $5700, the total amount that I saved (or contributed to) the museum over the past four years in volunteer work at $4.25 an hour. The party slowly dispersed. There were many congratulations, overwhelming happiness, excitement, and revelry.

In the near future, my relationship with Karmen blossomed. It was more intense, but was always innocent, pure, and respectful. We held hands everywhere we could, the exhibit about the aquatic life that lived under the docks in South Boston's channels that the museum rested on, we embraced in the multicultural exhibit, we made sure no one knew about the fact that we spent the final hour of the late Friday night's openings in one another's exhibits. In our arms. Most importantly, as the problems in my life that I had no control over intensified, the comfort and love that she would show me would also intensify.

She was an angel. *Ella, a mi ángel.*

I anticipated seeing her all of the time. I needed to.

As we grew older, her own issues began to evolve. Her father wouldn't allow her to date, go to dances with any boys let alone me, to socialize; but how thankful she was to be at the museum. With me.

She turned seventeen. She was older than me by two years, and it seemed like it was time for her to move on from the museum. She gave her two weeks notice, and since there was such an immediacy once I learned about this, my heart would race every time I saw her. Remembering when my mother embarrassed me at the health club, I created a plan in my head to kiss her. To embrace her. No. No I couldn't do that. To ask her to be my girlfriend. We were already in love, that was apparent. It shouldn't be that difficult, right?

But whenever I would see her, my plan on scooping her up and kissing her like a hero in an action movie was completely lost. My desire for her grew, and so did my nerves. My mouth would open, and my mind would trample on my lowly human self. I feared losing the safe harbor of her amazing eyes, her hands, her lips, her embraces. Her holy embraces. My innocence and respect for her transformed into a blockade of intense fleeting fear.

And so we came to that Friday night. The last Friday night. Her last Friday. Our last Friday. I finally had the guts to talk with her – I had to.

It was her break. She stopped in my exhibit to see me … we had not seen one another all night. The anxiety I felt was stifling. She was beautiful – wearing a white collared shirt under a tight vest. Her perfume, sweet and fresh. Her body. Her breasts. Her sophistication. It was late.

I walked her toward the break room while we chatted about incidental things. I sincerely felt as though my heart would explode out of my chest, what the hell was I thinking? I couldn't do this, and yet, this was my only chance.

While I don't remember what we talked about, this memory remained completely. It turned in my mind over, and over again, and was unforgettable. We were halfway up the industrial stairwell. We were alone. I stopped her. I took her hands. This was it.

"Karmen, I know your family is really strict, and everything, but... If I never asked you... I would regret it if I never asked you. Tonight. What would you say if I asked you to be my girlfriend?"

I wouldn't have been able to predict it. Above me on the stairs, she looked down at me, smiled, and replied, "I will have to think about it."

She walked away to the break room, and the more I began to think about it, the more neurotic I had started to become. What if her father came to kick my ass? What if her brother was in a gang, or even the boys at these dances she couldn't go to, and came to shoot me in the face for asking such a stupid question? What in god's name were you even thinking asking it, white boy? I would be shot in the face.

I felt panicky the whole rest of the night. When I spoke with coworkers, I constantly believed that our interactions were underscored by a blatant belief that they knew what I had finally had the guts to ask Karmen, and I would be the laughingstock of everyone. Whatever the result, I saw and finally accepted that this irreversible fuckup on my part would eventually lead to me learning something, even if it was how to pull my bloody, badly beaten corpse out of the gutter on my own for being a stupid white boy asking such a stupid, stupid question.

At the end of the night, she was scheduled to be in the exhibit that was meant for the visitors with infants and really young children. I was three exhibits down in the exhibit showcasing fifty or so vintage dollhouses under glass. It was almost time to go. I had to be sure I would see her. I had to see her. I had to get her phone number. I had to.

I went there. She wasn't there. I couldn't have missed her. She couldn't have left. The exhibits were empty, visitors were filing out, and announcements were being made telling people to exit. Thank you for coming. Make your way to the exits. Come again. The building was already empty.

It was nine. Closing time. Then nine-fifteen. I had to get to the train to get home, and if I missed it, I would be set back another hour waiting for the next one. I had to find Karmen before I left and she made her way home to East Boston. Somewhere. I didn't even know where she lived. In the shadow of the Madonna? Unique above all other creatures, beautiful, worthy of worship, this Karmen, my Karmen, she must live there. That would be my only option.

I thought about this as I walked, scanned the building, and I saw her on the second floor. She was walking toward me. In the exhibit about the sea life under the docks. She was cool. She was confident. She was grace.

"I have been looking for you!" A smile inched its way across her face. The dimple. A spark in my chest. "I have to go – my dad is downstairs. He is going to kill me. But I thought about it. My dad really wants me to be with the boys from church, or from the neighborhood, even though he really doesn't want me to be with any boys. But I don't care. Yes. That is my answer. Yes."

I couldn't believe what she said. I already wanted her so terribly badly. I wanted her close, and I wanted to fall asleep with her next to me. We hugged in the most truthful and tight embrace. It was amazing. She wrote her phone number down on the back of my work schedule, and she left quickly. I watched her walk away.

Days went by. I remember thinking that I wanted more than anything for this to work between us. This was different, and wasn't a crush or a lustful obsession. I began to analyze all of my previous relationships – there weren't many – but wondering how I could approach this perfectly. Utterly perfectly. If I called her too early, I would seem like a creep who can't wait one minute to be away from her. She hasn't even settled down from working so much and can't have even one free second for herself. What the hell was I thinking?

I began to practice my Spanish, in the event that it was all her parents spoke. Over and over I rehearsed the phone call, playing it over and over in my mind. What would I say? *¿Hola, es Karmen en casa?* How could I sound like a gentleman? *¿Puedo hablar con ella?* What would our date be like, and where would I take her? *¿Dónde la llevo? Cena ... Eso es todo. Voy a tener a su casa a las ocho.* How could I get her father to trust me right away? *No voy a dejar que le pase nada a su hija. Confía en mí.* To take his daughter from their house, under my supervision and show her a good time and have her back for curfew at the right hour? *Me dijo que ocho, señor. Me refiero a ocho.* I didn't know what the hell I was doing. *¿Qué demonios estaba pensando?*

The following week went by as if it were a normal one. Completely normal. School was a terrible waste of time – I continued to bomb my classes, I hung out with my friend Kevin and his girlfriend Sheryl, and I continued to go to work. But the Tuesday the followed that, I made sure my radio was off, my door was closed, my attention was strict, and my constitution and focus was surgically trained on speaking with Karmen.

I dialed.

It rang.

A man's voice answered.

"Hello?" English. I was taken aback because I had done so much preparation. But this would not be a complete embarrassment.

"Hello, is Karmen there?"

"Who is this?"

"This is... a friend, from the museum."

Now, I don't particularly remember how the next part of the conversation went from there, but what I do remember is that the man, presumably her father, hung up on me. I sat on the bed, my heart pounding, and hung up the phone.

...And I never called back.

Time drifted past from that moment on. I completely changed eventually, but first I burned up through the eighth and ninth grades. I managed to survive it, and was reborn like the phoenix in the tenth grade. In high school, I managed to 'get' school, and I was getting exceptional grades. I coasted through my courses.

I had a lot to show for my accomplishments. I graduated with honors, I had written a thesis, I even managed to make it into the top quarter of the graduating class. I had a band, a resume of some pretty attractive girlfriends, and a few very close friends. But at this moment I realized that the one thing I didn't have was the opportunity to share it with Karmen.

The years passed so quickly, and along with elements of my existence began to develop my personal philosophy. My tastes developed. I look back as the present day me and I feel that my philosophy, my tastes, and even many of my decisions were uneducated and foolish. But I was a child. I was a populist. Regardless, the development since created a personality and a desire to succeed. I was taken by an unflinching desire to make things happen, to be aware of more. To simplify and to learn. To experience. But one thing did not change – no matter the direction I was headed in, I began to be reminded of the hunger that I felt for

Karmen – to have that amazing relationship I deserved and the fulfillment of what I was missing. To close the current chapter with my girlfriend April, and to open the new chapter with Karmen.

I was to begin college at Wentworth Institute of Technology in Boston. Karmen was in Boston. I still loved Karmen. It was almost too easy and made too much sense. She was probably more beautiful than ever, and just as lonely. What the hell was I doing here, feeling so alone, missing a piece of my life that she had fulfilled so selflessly.

One night, soon after the graduation parties and the reality of life free from school had begun to set in, I picked up the phone and dialed the familiar number that had sat in the same place on my desk where I had left it so long ago.

"Hello?" A woman's voice.

"Hi, is Karmen there?"

"Who?"

"Karmen Calderon."

"I am sorry, I think you have the wrong number."

...I paused. I repeated the number back to her.

"Yes. Sorry, no Karmen."

I couldn't believe her. I do not know why, or what happened, or how this could be even true. "Did they move, or is – do you live in East Boston?"

"No, we've had this number for a while. No Karmen has

ever lived here... I am so sorry."

I had hit a wall, and I told the woman on the phone my entire story. I felt like crying. I had no idea why it was so important to keep this stranger on the phone. Her patience waned. I ended the conversation. I sat and thought.

That night, before I had to leave for work I pulled out my credit card from the back of my wallet. I was going to find one of those websites that would find anyone for a small fee. It was eight dollars. I typed in Karmen Calderon. I clicked search.

There were seven names, phone numbers, and addresses that came up. Calderon. East Boston. I hand wrote seven notes, addressed them, and sent them in the mail. In them, my story was the same – I was graduating high school, looking for my lost friend who meant a tremendous amount to me – helped me survive to this point that I was now graduating high school and was going to college. I put an email address I set up just for that purpose, and asked them to please contact me whether they were who I was looking for or not.

The subtext was even more painful. That I would someday hope that I would reconnect and somehow convince her that it was her that I was living for. That I was hopefully going to see her and she would be proud of me. That it was my fault I never saw her again. That I miss her so goddamn much that I feel it before I go to bed every day, that I would lie awake and whisper her name in the dark, and that there wasn't a day that went by that I did not think about her.

And then the responses came in. They were unanimous.

"I am sorry. I am not your Karmen. Good luck in your search."

My eight dollars were spent in vain, and it seemed for a while that I was completely without any semblance of her. It eventually became true. Hope became my enemy, as it was in so many other avenues of my life. I considered going to Montel Williams' website, or Maury Povich. I considered writing an appeal to be on one of their reunion shows where they hire private investigators and truly find that person that I was so desperately searching for. To tell the whole country on live television how wonderful she was to me. How much she meant to me...

The cameras would slide across the studio floor, the lights would come up, and the host would smile.

"Boy have we got a surprise for you. We have a wonderful, amazing, true surprise for you. Ladies and gentleman, the woman that this young man has been looking for has been living not two blocks away from him, also on Huntington Avenue since she moved out of her parents house. Here she is, Ms. Karmen Calderon!"

The crowd would cheer, and my eyes would be fixated on the door in the set, and she would emerge, and she would be the most beautiful and amazing creature I had ever set eyes on. The moment our eyes connected, we would have nothing left but to run at each other. Throw ourselves at one another. To literally smash into one another so violently that we fell over, crying, crying tears of joy and embracing on the floor. Could we get any closer, goddamnit? Melt us! The eyes of the host and the cameras and everyone around searching for some way that this could be captured on camera. Do we have a camera that could get this? Are you getting this? And all we can think is love, love, love.

■ ■ ■

Standing in line at graduation, I reflected on the elemental forces such as the one that is humming in the back of my mind at this moment, the constant yearning for home. I reflect on the past me, and I want to tell that fourteen year old me that everything will be okay, and that ultimately there was nothing that he needed to worry about.

I wanted to tell him that shortly after my twenty-eighth birthday, I was going to receive my master's degree. That would be after my bachelor's degree in 2004. That I would go to college, even, and be able to afford it. That eventually I will get laid, and not to worry about women except that I should really be worried about what my priorities are. That I should try to remember everything, and keep a journal. That I should study more. That I should let Mom fight her own demons, because ultimately, she was the one that needed to change herself. It would be okay. We'd all make it.

I often wondered what it would be like to have a reunion of the teens of the Teen Jobs Program. I wanted to embrace the strict nostalgia that I had for those times, and I hoped that everyone was safe, happy, and successful. I could say that I recognize myself being who I am in part because of the way that they were with me. I hold that so very close.

I also understood that this fantasy that I had devised was a result of my understanding of human nature that I have developed, along with my concept of the world. What I had recognized is that it could be so much worse, so much worse to face the circumstances of my reality as a bystander to the tragedy of my past existence.

But it was so much easier to look back and imagine that episode of of the talk show. How things would have been different...

It was six months of communication with the producers of

the program that went by before it was to be filmed, practically a lifetime since they began. I meet Mr. Povich, an admirable man and a figurehead of multiculturalism and equality in America. I tell him this - "Maury! A Jew, married to an Asian American, both of you broadcasting giants! You are amazing!" - and we shake hands. His handshake is strong, mature, respectful. He leads me to the green room, and there is a young man with a radio headset with me, waiting until it is time, when he will lead me to the sound stage.

I gorge myself on pastries and bagels on the food services cart. The intern gets the signal, and communicating through various hand gestures, I follow him down a series of narrow hallways and stand behind the plywood door that leads onto the set. Maury mentions my name, the intern pats me on the back, and I am immediately thrust in front of a few hundred complimentary ticket holders and I take a seat on Maury's couch.

"Welcome," he would say, "everyone here is so really proud to have someone as inspirational as you here. Do tell us your story," and I would. From the beginning. As I recounted everything that happened, the audience would be rapt in what I say, cameras cutting to them recounting their own lives, some sniffling into tissues and some sobbing. Where were their own lost loves now?

But I had an advantage. I must know that she is here, now, just waiting backstage! I have rehearsed this in my mind for ages! Yes! This must be true! This must be really happening! Right Now! Aren't You Paying Attention, Fuckers? This is the real thing!

"Well," he would segue, "we had gotten your story along with hundreds of others in the mail, and yours was particularly compelling because of the great impact that this young woman made on your life. I want to tell you that we were able to track Karmen down and we want to bring you two together today." My eyes dart around in my head. Are you serious, Maury? Right now? I,...I can't even believe this! Where is she? "Karmen has no idea why she is with us today, so, please everyone, give a huge round of applause to Ms. Karmen Calderon!"

The world would clap and cheer, and Karmen would walk, pre-scripted in her direction and purpose, down the opposite ramp and toward the sofas. She would give Maury a hug and sit down next to me on the sofa.

"Do you know why you are here, Karmen?" He asked her in a hopeful, magical manner.

"No..." She looks at me out of the corner of her eye, quickly to the audience, and then back to Maury. She is smiling. The dimple in her top lip has not changed with time, age, or anything. She illuminates the room. She was absolutely beautiful.

"You are here to reacquaint yourself, and us here in the audience, with an old friend. This old friend has spent countless hours thinking and reflecting on what an impact you have had on his life," camera cut to various introspective faces in the audience. "a man whose life you changed for the better in the face of a great deal of adversity he faced as an adolescent. Karmen, do you know who is sitting next to you right now?"

The crowd would stay silent, in stasis, anticipating her response. She looks at me, her eyes luminous. She searches and searches every angle and aspect of it for something that was recognizable.

"...No,...No, Maury. I am sorry." The first blow. Was it utter denial, or was it truly the fact that there was simply no recognition of any facet of us? Our existence?

"This young man has just told us an amazing and romantic story of your relationship that you had in the mid-nineteen nineties that was cut short by some terribly sad and unfortunate twists of fate that cut you off from one another for at least the past fifteen years!" The photo of the birthday party is shown on the large screen behind the sofa. "Does this look familiar?"

"Is that... Oh, The Children's Museum!"

"It is. And the young man there in the middle was celebrating his birthday-"

"Oh!" She would look at me, "oh... oh, yes! Oh, I remember you!"

And that would be it. The magic of the moment, and the element of surprise, and the approach of the recognition of all things wonderful would...actually vanish. We would finish a light conversation on camera, and we would never see one another again. She not only didn't remember me, but I was nothing to her. My fire became a small, stifled spark. The light dimmed. We were something that was never there. A magic trick.

■ ■ ■

I walked with the rest of my graduating classmates into the humid auditorium, searching for familiar faces. I immediately saw my mother. My sister. My wife and her mother. My good friend Jim. They ushered in this new chapter of my life along with me, beaming with smiles, joyful, unashamed and proud. Lovely. The moment was wonderful.

I stood. I was recognized and hooded. I received my diploma. I sat. I thought about those old moments, and these new moments, and they came and went like smoke.

The next afternoon, mom came over the house and had dinner with us. As I cooked, mom went out to her car to retrieve some forgotten items. She brought back several boxes of old family photos. Many were painful memories that were jarring, and what was most notable were the years that there were absolutely no photos or evidence that we existed at all. There were more pictures of her at work, actually her students, than there were of us. I was somehow okay with that. There were images of her trip to North Dakota with my sister and that student of hers that was living at our house at the time. In the photos were burly, leather-clad bikers with their topless wenches on the back of their bikes, hurling down the highway toward Sturgis for their yearly gathering. There were photos of Mount Rushmore, historical societies, free city museums filled with bizarre western nostalgia and folklore.

We sat at the table and flipped through these visual artifacts. The photographs passed. The bikers, the elderly, the smiles, the skin... Something about these images called to me and instructed me that most of them were dead now. Many of the dogs, the buffalo, and the big breasted women on the back of motorcycles, hair flowing in the 70 mph wind and desert freeway, boobs mid-bounce, frozen in a happier time. Why in hell did Mother take this picture?

The hamburgers we ate were delicious, although they were my own recipe and I made them often. We feasted on juicy grilled ground beef, looking through the photos, and enjoyed our company. My wife looked at the photos of my sister in her awkward years, touristy clothing, bug-bite-breasts all the way through her rebellious cigarette-widow, dead to the world in eye makeup years. My friend Jim admired my mother's suffering, beauty, and lost years. Mom and my sister reflected on the wild lifestyles of the bikers and their wives and lovers.

And then...

And then in an aside...

And then in an aside Mother mentioned...

"Oh... Here is an old photo from the Museum... I am not sure if you even – whatever...."

She shuffled it back into a stack of photographs of no historical or personal attachment to me whatsoever.

"Wait, what?" I gestured that she hand me the picture.

It was washed out. Instant camera. Reflective and hazy. Askew. It was a representation of what was certainly one of the greatest days of my life. The lighting was horrible. In the middle was my smiling face, dorky in the middle of a sea of faces. It was the very photograph. The very one that I thought was lost so long ago.

It was terrible.

The lens, unpolished and foggy. Half of the faces were faded into obscurity. Those of us with darker skin were hardly even visual, they only remained as specters and outlines – nothingness - or a shine of a light bouncing off their faces. The camera was fucking racist. Some of the girls in the photo were not even smiling – you wouldn't even suggest that they were aware that their picture was being taken if it weren't for the others in the picture. Obviously they were posing. Right?

In the center was my smiling face, flanked by a very good friend, Nancy, and Daniel a new found acquaintance had either started on a poor note or ended on one. Behind me to the right, one of the supervisors, Joanna, was giving me bunny ears. To my left,

Karmen was giving Daniel bunny ears.

There was disappointment. But out of the photo and its disappointment was also an intense appreciation. While it was, in fact a terrible picture, while it did the moment absolutely no justice and certainly didn't exist on the plane of my memory of the day at all,... Karmen. Karmen remained beautiful and committed and amazing in that picture. Her youth and happiness was a beacon through the years, shining through her eyes, burning a hole in the paper.

Disappointment still remained there, for the present day me. Here. Now. There was no question that this was the photograph that I longed for so readily; that I thought about so many times. But it nearly wasn't as wonderful as I remembered it. As a matter of fact, it was, as they say, shitty.

The memory of the photo was so much more vivid, much more lucid and visceral than this flimsy and arguably depressing picture of a young man and his improvised birthday party that was attended and organized by himself and his friends. A bunch of city kids. And I began to remember how ghetto my life seemed at the time. My family had nothing. We shopped at the thrift store. I accompanied friends to the free clothes in the basements of churches, and we would laugh as we chose clothing, but underneath we seriously gazed out of the corner of our eyes at everything in hopes we would find something we needed. Needed.

Everything seemed cheap. Even my friendships, really. I was burning out, and I was such a burnout because I mostly spent my time with burnouts. It was tragic and brutal. I considered joining the army so that I wouldn't perpetuate this cycle of failure. I had nothing left.

And what the hell was I thinking?

If the present day me could have just gone back to tell the past-self that everything would be okay! If I could have told that self to take that girl's face into your hands and kiss her more passionately than anything that you had ever believed in. She was a salvation – she was the representation of everything better to me. Why the fuck don't you do something about her? She will change your life! You will survive this and make it! In fifteen years you will be living in a beautiful place and have a beautiful wife and a dog and you will live in the woods. You will love it! But now you need to study. You need to take care of yourself and not worry so much. Mom? She is on her own journey. Ditch the old burnout friends. You really need to kiss that girl.

There was a terrible tragedy within this whole thing. The terrible tragedy is that there was absolutely nothing I could say to the past self to make him understand just how lucky he would be. Nothing! I could see a terrible hyphen at the end of every word I would say to him - of every sentence. I would see my suited, sharp looking self examined by this grungy teen that I was: taking in the look that I perpetuated. This vision that I was is simple: something I told myself that I would never become. Would there be no comfort in that?

No. There wouldn't.

I would still go home to my alcoholic mother every night and envision myself smashing all of her bottles on the floor of the garage to point out her complete ineptitude of looking at life as what it really was. I would still waste away afternoons with Kevin and Sheryl in hopes that I might someday get into her pants. Her pants, and his pants, and everyone's pants were just so dysfunctional. Just like mine. There was an understanding in that regardless of the actual utter passion and comfort I felt with Karmen. There was a fear I had for Karmen. There was the carelessness I had for school. There was the absolutely crippling examination of existence rather than self.

There would be nothing different. But then, I wondered – the end result will then have to change if I changed before it was time. The time that I changed was easy to explicate. When I was a sophomore in high school, years later when I virtually forgot about all of this, my cousin moved in with us for a short time from far away. One of the few times his father, my uncle, dropped him off, he left me with a book. *Share the Joy*, by Colin Higgins. I later learned it was a novelization of the film Higgins wrote, *Harold and Maude*. I read the book in one sitting. I watched the film. Immediately, my relationship with Kevin, with Sheryl, all ended tumultuously. I was destroyed. I was reborn. Years later, married with child at my grandfather's funeral, I asked my uncle if he remembered giving the book to me. He didn't.

Would things have been different? In a word, no. In a sense, no. Even if I was able to get through to that adolescent me. Even if I got through and made such an impression on that self, even if it stuck for some reason, all I would have to show for it was a selfish and headstrong Hal, awaiting the throne that I was promised. I wouldn't be here, and I certainly wouldn't be me, and I certainly wouldn't be happy. If I met that other me, today, I would hate him for his arrogance and his nature. Instead, I remained closest to Falstaff.

As these occasions continued to arise in my life, I learned to be ready for them. It seemed that while I loved before and after, that one remained pure. Easy. The wordless kind of vindication. The innocent sleep. The beautiful ring of my tree that indicates that time period would have been just as painful and scarred, but healed by her innocent touch.

The lovely tragedy of the silence that existed since then is that you cannot ever go home; you can never visit this home or even consider any aspect of it – the memory of the photo was so much sweeter than the actual photograph itself. Until it arose again, halfheartedly from a pile in a suitcase, it remained frozen in time and perfect, as did Karmen and everyone else. I am certain that the memory of those moments simply rely on a nostalgia that is so much sweeter than the factual aspects of these moments.

Until we can go home, there is nothing to do but love.

The Halcyon Library

The telephone rang in her pocket and the black feeling in the depths of Amanda's stomach meant only that it was Chandler. She thought of him. His smiling visage. His affluence. His embrace. As much as her best friend insisted she completely forget about the man, to use the pain and torment of their breakup as the whetstone of her anger, she tended to invest in this feeling of the deepest, darkest brown bile reaching up for her heart. For some reason the dark emptiness was comforting, especially on the recurring lonely nights filling her days.

She looked at the telephone deep in her pocketbook. The ring was set to "Marionette." Garfunkel. They would listen to "Watermark" in the conservatory on vinyl. The candles, the eery soft voice, the dancing, the echo; it was always so intoxicating and comforting late at night. She wondered why she fell into the pit of this memory. If she answered it, like she should, she could talk to him. But then she would feel obligated to tell her girlfriends about it, because she had promised that she wouldn't do that. She had three more bars of music to decide.

The innocence of her trust in everyone had been relatively acceptable, if not naive. Until about a year ago when they had first met, her drastic desperation consumed her. She needed anyone to sleep next to, needed excitement, needed to find fun in the mundane and beauty in the world.

The account on the Internet dating site helped, "white creative pixie in search of laughter and fun." Fifty responses, low quality, dull, pudgy, balding, and the worst part, her own horrible high expectations. The week later, "intriguing brunette, in search of an intellectual." No responses. An unrealistic exercise in finding something sophisticated, and yet her girlfriends insisted.

But when she arrived at the weekly poetry reading in the new gallery and community art space in downtown Amherst, she never imagined that she would be explaining to her girlfriends over dinner that she met a man. A rich man. A real, tall, dark, handsome, and sophisticated man at a real public, offline event... in reality.

"Like, as in, real life? What, did you schedule a meet up or something?" Sarah practically knocked her chardonnay into everyone's quinoa.

"What? No. I met him there. Totally random." The three women at the table's expressions, mouths agape, were as solid as a tree trunk. Karen had even stopped looking at her phone to see if her husband had killed their child for five seconds to focus her attention on Amanda.

"So... so you met a guy? Go, go, go on!" Karen was the first person to break the silence.

"Well," Amanda began, "I was at the poetry reading to check out that new space, and – well, you know how I am always looking for things to do. So, I am sitting there, and listening, and it is great, and there is this guy sitting at the end of the row, staring at me. He has a suit on, a shock of gray hair – actually, that he is too young for, not because he is old, just, sort of like, Steve Martin, I guess? - and also he is tall, and strong. He came to talk to me during the intermission, and we decided to go over his house for some wine after the show."

While Amanda explained the situation in a manner consistent with her personality, as if she were outlining the newest recipe for the delicious raspberry tequila squares she brought to the party, the table was much more receptive to this news which lay in front of them with such heft no one could lift their forks to continue eating.

She continued, "and then back at his place, which is a huge three-story mansion near the hospital, which I could only think that he picked up at the height of the downturn, we drank wine and listened to his records. The place is so cool, and I hope you can see it some day because there are books everywhere. I mean, *everywhere*. Every wall is a bookshelf. So we had cheese, and danced, and then he drove me home... I have gone over a few more times since then, and have had a really nice time. His cook, or chauffeur, or his servant, or concierge – I don't know what he is called, he seems to do it all – has been picking me up and dropping me off at home on his own way home every night. It has been pretty cool. He is a really great guy."

The women were confused. Utterly confused. Willa thought, 'the crazy cat lady has finally found a catch.' Sabina thought, 'what is this? I am supposed to be finding rich, healthy men, and when I do I will stick my claws in so deep. She is going to mess this up entirely.' Sarah thought, well, she thought nothing. This was unparalleled. Karen was the only one who was genuinely happy, and could not wait to listen to her stories and allow her imagination to run vicariously wild.

"Did you kiss him yet?" Karen asked.

"No... No, it has only been a week, really." Their brows then crinkled up. They began thinking this man was gay. Or married and his wife was just away. Those were the only explanations.

"What does he do?" Sarah asked.

"He is a writer. A self made man, evidently, but I tried to find his books at the store and they aren't there. So, I suppose he just had one hit and it made him rich or something, and he has just kept everything he's written? Or he uses a different name? I don't really want to ask yet."

The women ate the rest of their meals in silence.

As the next five months continued, Amanda grew so much more impressed by this amazing man's home, and his servant, and his Rolls Royce; but the only thing that she wanted to know more about was his work. Every night she was invited over and picked up she would immediately find ways to nonchalantly make her way over to one of the bookshelves, but whenever she did, she was immediately interrupted. Or dinner was ready. Or it was time to move from the drawing room to the conservatory to listen to his newest vintage Japanese import Herb Alpert record or dance, or to the cellar to open a old bottle of sherry for no apparent reason but to be romantic and impressive.

Unfortunately Amanda was always a bibliophile, and these games began to irritate the itch that formed in her palms and on the back of her neck. It was as if the leaves of books were the cool, soft damp cloths soaked with calamine and rubbing alcohol that mother would massage into her summer poison ivy rashes she'd get on her ten-year-old tomboy adventures.

So, the moment came when Amanda had a particularly long week, and sitting down with one of her own books in Chandler's conservatory with some soft classical music playing and the promise of a light dinner sounded exquisite. She had given up on the idea of her face being taken in his hands, touched with an amazing kiss, and it began to feel natural to just be comfortable and happy in his company. She liked him, but it had been six months; if she couldn't be satiated in one way, she must in another.

"I was thinking a dinner of Cornish hen and a couple of refreshing Mojitos on the patio would be wonderful on a warm night like tonight. I could put my Sibelius on the record player," Chandler began, in his masculine and sophisticated way. Amanda cut him off.

"-I really would like to just sit and be comfortable. Dinner sounds great, and the music, but could we... Read? Be together and just get comfortable and maybe you and I could grab one of your books, maybe? I'm sorry, but I've just had a long week." It wasn't until it was out that Amanda realized she sounded whiny and ungrateful.

"I'm afraid that's out of the question, Amanda."

She was confused about his response, but the power of his words made her breath melt onto her stomach. Was this an order of some kind? She was fine with his original plan, but she was afraid that if she did not take action that the relationship would be just the eating of rich food and fine music and wines. At his house. Full of books. Water, water everywhere, but not a drop to drink. She mustered a response.

"Well, I mean, that's okay. You're a writer, after all, and I just figured we could spend some time together-"

"No." Masculine and direct.

So, they spent their night with music, dancing, and muted revelry on the patio. But as Amanda danced, she devised that she would excuse herself to use the restroom, and slyly take one of the volumes from the shelf with her. The plan wasn't brilliant, well thought out, or even complete, but this was the turning point where she would make some sense of this man who seemingly was stringing her along for months. This was it. She made the decision that it was to be after the song had finished playing; any minute considering the song had been playing for roughly twenty minutes. One record side could only hold so much, after all.

The symphony died down, and the record turned to crackles and pops. He bowed. She curtsied.

"Excuse me," she said, and began toward the house.

"Amanda?" She turned. Out of nowhere, he was upon her. One strong, muscular hand had reached up to her jaw, and the other grabbed her behind the neck. The feeling that came next was a wave of explosive water, electric fire. He was strong, but gentle. He kissed her, and she fell into the cobbled patio and melted between the cracks of the stones.

It seemed that her mind had been made up for her, their lips never stopped touching and the waves carried them upstairs into his bedroom for hours. Daylight had been gone for hours, and the candles danced along the walls just as the sheets danced in the breeze. They slept, dreamless and relaxed. Contentment, comfort, and relaxation absorbed into their bones.

When she awoke at three-thirty in the morning, his warm hand remained on her hip. She had to use the bathroom.

She stepped out of the four post bed, and walked over to the floor to ceiling french doors that were opened out to a stone porch. The wind made the air shift and bulge the beautiful and luminous silk curtains. The air, the view, the property; it was all beautiful, symmetrical, and perfect. The moon was full, and bravely shone on the land below. The grass sparkled with dew.

Amanda turned back, and walked out into the hallway. She

was smiling in the dark house. She walked twenty paces, and put her hand out to the right to feel for where the door began. Instead, she felt books. The thought suddenly hit her; the night before, she never followed through with her plan to take a book from the shelf as an excuse to use the bathroom. This was the moment; as good as any. A pee and a quick read, and then back to bed.

She found the doorway, and pulled a tome from the shelf without looking. She closed the door behind her, turned on the light, put the seat down, and examined the volume in her hands. Bound in brown leather the book looked like an artifact, but it was much too new to be antique. The pages and binding looked unread, uncracked, uncut, and new. She smelled it. Leather? Oil? No. It was distinct. Musky, and coppery. It was a new masterpiece, almost as if the text itself contained within was worthy of this fine craftsmanship that had not been seen for at least a century. What on earth was this?

The cover was a gilded design. It was a naked woman, not uncommon for books of this type with a particular Victorian-Era American air about them. She had sprites and vines spread around her, but most striking was her face. Usually expressionless, she noticed that this woman was almost wincing in pain. She was in a subdued agony. Then on second look, above her head her hands were bound by the vines that crept up around her. It actually almost looked as though the sprites or fairies were tormenting her. It looked as if the vines had terrible thorns on them. How curious, Amanda thought.

She turned the book to its spine.

"HEATHER, by Chandler W. LaCroix"

One of his books?

She turned it back to its pages, and slowly opened it in the center. The words were there, but they were hard to read. She knew she was reading English, that there was English on the page, but the words in front of her, frankly all of the English language no longer made any sense. The black ink turned to brown, then to red, and then the ink began to bleed out of itself. The copper smell was louder in her nose. The letters O, D, Q just closed up and pooled over, as did the others. The liquid ran down the page and into her legs. She removed a hand holding the book, and tried to wipe it away, but it was sticky and syrupy. It wouldn't move, and yet it kept coming, drooling everywhere, bleeding over itself.

It was blood.

It was pooling in a river in the center of the book, and beginning to rush quicker and quicker from it, and a rivulet formed from the spine of the book in between her legs and up her lap. In horror, she stood and dropped it. It landed with a hard 'pack' and spread open to the center. The right side pages almost looked cut away, like a book safe, and within the blood that was now pouring out of it was a heart, veiny and beating. She felt as if it were staring right at her.

She ran from the bathroom, slipping in the sticky, congealing gore on her feet. Right out of the bathroom, left down the grand staircase, and through the front door. She was two steps onto the front porch until she realized she was still naked, and turned back quickly into the house to retrieve her purse and her dress, all left strewn in the conservatory off of the main hall where they had left all of their clothes.

The moon illuminated the bookshelf directly opposite her as she was reaching down to retrieve her clothes. The gilt lettering reflected back, "JOHANNA, Chandler W. LaCroix," "PAIGE, Chandler W. LaCroix," "VALERIE, Chandler W. LaCroix." There were hundreds of books. Thousands of books.

She didn't even stay to change, but chose to run out of the house, and kept running nude and bloody down the woody street of mansions and affluence in the middle of the night. She would have screamed the entirety of the way if she didn't need the breath. Eventually, she slowed. She had stopped under a street light to put her clothes on, and then kept moving toward Old Brook Road. When she arrived at Karen's it was already five in the morning. The grim horror wore off, and the grim reality set in.

She rang the doorbell. Karen's husband Todd opened the door, with baby Elemina on his hip. He had already been up.

"Amanda. Wow, uh, was Karen expecting you?" His face was tired, and unsure of what he was looking at.

"I am sorry, I – I look awful, but I didn't do it. Could you just – could you go get her?" She was exhausted, drained, and defeated.

Todd disappeared into the house. Karen returned in a robe, not entirely awake until she saw Amanda.

"Oh, my god, Amanda, come in!"

"I'm so sorry, I have no idea what happened. I look like a monster. This blood isn't mine."

"What?" Karen was confused. Amanda looked tousled and unkempt, as if she was destroyed or raped. She put her arm around Amanda and walked her into the house. She sat her on the sofa. "No, what happened? Do we need to call the police? Or go to the hospital?"

"What? No. No... I don't think so. I just walked from Chandler's, but I am okay. He didn't do anything,... I don't think. I could use a shower and some sleep."

"Sure, Amanda, whatever you need."

So, she ran the shower. As steam filled the room, she examined herself in the mirror. No blood. Nothing. Regardless of her cleanliness, she felt filthy. She bathed, and then refreshed and exhausted, she went to the guest room and slept.

Almost immediately she dreamed of walking through Chandler's house, but it wasn't Chandler's house the way it looked. It was a warehouse, with industrial shelf after industrial shelf of books. The lighting was horrible – dim, and half lit. Some bulbs were burnt out, and some had only half of the electricity they needed. They hummed and blinked.

Amanda walked through the stacks, and along with the humming was the sickly slap of her feet landing on the floor. It was concrete where she started, but eventually was coated in a thin, sticky veneer of blood. Her feet sucked it up in tendrils as she lifted them. Tak, tak, tak. She noticed that the blood dripped in rivulets to the floor from the shelves like spilled honey.

And then the sound of the books breathing; beating.

She began to walk faster, but the sticky, slippery blood made it hard to keep a foothold.

And then the screaming began, like hundreds of pages being torn, but also hundreds of women's voices beginning glass-shattering gaspy screams of horror. Pops, cracks, the whispy whisper of fire, and she turned and the books were ablaze. Bloody, bold, burning, the names went up, and the fire and the books burned. The blood was like oil. The smoke was suffocating.

She began to run, and the blood slipped further beneath her feet. It was hard to run, and scary. Scary not only for the running, but now she noticed that she was naked, and didn't want to land in the lake collecting at her feet. Then her ankles. It was changing.

She saw a door ahead with an industrial waterproof dock light above it. The blood would drown her if she didn't get out of there. The rivulets began to drip up her legs, in creamy red lines opposite of the way the blood fell from the shelves. It covered her legs, and up to her waist, and she was disgusted, and horrified, the gore sliding up her. She would drown and burn.

When she had made it to the door, she was relieved to find it unlocked. The blood splashed aside when she opened it, and she shoved it closed behind her. Blackness. She turned on the light. It was a bathroom, industrial with hand tiled floor, and stainless steel. In the mirror, Amanda was reflected clean and white; again, no blood. She slid down the door, and sat.

That is when she heard Chandler whisper in her ear, "you're mine now."

When she awoke with the tingling sensation of his breath on her neck, she noticed Karen and her husband had left. She showered and went home, and it was at six that night that she learned Karen had set up an emergency girls meeting. They descended on her apartment unannounced, and told Amanda that she was never to see or speak to this man again. She agreed – as a matter of fact the level of her enthusiasm was comforting to her friends – and that was that.

Over the next six months, she received typed letters from Chandler. They all amounted to the same thing, beautiful poetic love letters that she amassed and read with eagerness. They opened with "My Dearest Amanda," and always contained the obligatory "I need you," "I love you," "Where have you been, but in my dreams?," "How could I have scared you off? We are magic." He would also call, and leave messages. "Dear, dear Amanda, I so desperately need to see you. To feel you in my arms and to kiss you. Why won't you return my letters or my phone calls? At least tell me what I've done!"

But she couldn't.

She couldn't do anything but reread the masterfully penned letters, and save her messages and listen to them over and over again. She felt owned, and she enjoyed it. She felt as if this man, this writer, was doing nothing less than weaving her into his writing and making her name a part of his words. Every time she was able to consume his letters and his voice mails, she could not help it but become enamored with his words. His use, his form, his possession of her name in his handwriting or his voice. Amanda, Amanda, Amanda.

Every week that went by she began to think to herself, this is the week that I will finally pick up the phone, answer the letter, call his driver to come and retrieve me. Every week however, she understood that by doing this, she may very well be inviting herself to the empty warehouse of books to hide from her friends that love her so dearly. So, her online dating account lay dormant, and she filled her nights with thoughts of the affluent and charming gentleman who held her heart. She ate with her friends, married with children, and spent her nights alone in her bed contemplating how the stars brought them together so explosively. Romantically. Chandler, and fate, owned Amanda.

Dinner, drinks, friends. The repeat story of the past five celibate years, and her phone rings in her purse. Her phone, that only rang on the most pressing of occasions. She looked down in her lap as Sarah was recounting her boyfriend's foray into laundry, ruining all of her bras when he put them in the dryer on the towel setting. In her lap was her purse. In her purse was her phone. She opened it like a small book, even though she knew who was calling. Chandler.

She so desperately needed to hear his voice. To see his smile, smell the expensive cologne and feel completely as though she could give her entire self to him and not feel in control. Feel as though someone else could be in control of her everything. That she can just give in. Give him the opportunity to finish that book he was working on that she could be a part of. His energy. His body. His oeuvre.

She excused herself from the table, and her girlfriends watched as she walked toward the bathroom. "Marionette." Two bars left. She entered, and walked straight into a stall. One bar. She pressed the answer button on her phone. She said the same words that Chandler had just finished typing onto the sheet of paper in his study.

And she was gone.

About the Author

Solomon Deep was born in 1969 in Memphis, and currently spends his time between New York and Northampton.

He is best known as the creator, producer, and head writer for the weekly live radio program Fortnight. Elements was his first published novel followed by several novels and collections produced and released by independent publishers.

Deep is a dedicated writer, poet, beekeeper, gardener, actor, and traveler.

128